CODE NAME:

HACKER

By
SAWYER BENNETT

D1160281

ISBN: 978-1-947212-85-5

Find Sawyer on the web!
sawyerbennett.com
www.twitter.com/bennettbooks
www.facebook.com/bennettbooks

Contents

CHAPTER 1

Griffin

EVEN THOUGH THE moon is at its fullest and brightest, there's enough cloud cover for me to stand at the edge of the woods behind the woman's house without being noticed. She lives about twenty miles north of the city of Pittsburgh in a little town called Cranberry.

I've learned a bit about her because I've been watching her for a few days. Her home is not modest. Cranberry is not as quaint as the name might infer, but affluent. Her house is a four-thousand-square-foot dwelling all done in gray brick with cream shutters and a manicured lawn. The suburban lifestyle is at odds with her day job, which I haven't quite figured out yet. When I followed her to work, she disappeared into an abandoned warehouse in a rundown section of Pittsburgh where she stayed until the evening commute home.

She's in her kitchen now, the window facing outward to her backyard. There's a massive child's playset in it that includes a slide, swings, fort, and a climbing wall.

Her kid is too old for it, and he never uses it. He does like to tromp through the woods, though. His trail leads down to a tiny creek where he valiantly tries to fish, but he comes up empty-handed because he doesn't know what he's doing. He clearly needs someone to show him a thing or two.

I study the woman, wondering how someone so pretty ended up in such a bad mess. She's petite, almost delicate, with exquisite bone structure. Her hair is so black it glints almost blue under the kitchen lighting. While the exact color of her eyes is not discernable from this distance, they are pale against the darkness of her hair. It makes her seem almost ethereal. Contrast that with the tattoos she has down her arms, and it adds an element of toughness in the way she holds herself. A steel spine is how I'd describe it.

She has tattoos in other places, too—ribs, legs, and back. I don't know that from watching her, though.

It's in the file back in my hotel room.

When I'd received it from my boss, it had been fairly thin and contained a photo that doesn't remotely resemble the woman I see now. She was young, in her early twenties, with bleached-blond hair cut extremely short, but she has one of those faces made for that style. There had even been a diamond stud in her nose, a ring in her lip, and a barbell through an eyebrow.

Blue. Pale, icy blue is the actual color of her eyes. I

can't quite see them through the cover of night, but they'd been vivid in that photo.

It was a prison photo, no doubt, and right below was a list of the tattoos she had with more close-up photos attached. They were meant to be used to identify her.

I was given her name, which is Bebe Grimshaw—formally known as Brianna Belle Grimshaw—and told to find her. My boss had heard through his underground network of black-market contacts that she was in the Pittsburgh area. With a little digging, I'd found her through the real estate tax records here in Cranberry.

I'm not the kind of employee—thug, muscle, hired help, or *whatever*—who does a half-assed job. I fleshed out the file I'd been given with some research of my own. Turns out Bebe Grimshaw had more of a colorful past than I ever could have imagined.

About eight years ago, she pled guilty to cyber-espionage charges leveled against her by the federal government. Seems the little fairy waif is incredibly talented at hacking, and she'd managed to pilfer nuclear codes that were in turn going to be sold to the Chinese. While that makes her far more interesting than the suburban single mom of a young boy who lives with her mother, what really interests me was how she refused to name any of her co-conspirators and was the lone person to take the fall for the crime.

She was sentenced to thirty-five years in prison.

Most would wonder how in the hell she's now living a quiet life in Cranberry, Pennsylvania, but I'm fairly sure I know the answer.

Given the things I've seen during the past two years of working for my boss, I'm going to take a pretty good guess he was involved in the nuclear-code hack.

As if thinking about the man procures him into reality, the phone in my pocket starts vibrating. I step several feet back into the tree line before turning my back on the Grimshaw home so the glow of my cell doesn't catch Bebe's interest while she finishes the dinner dishes.

The man's name is programmed into my contacts as simply AB, which stands for Anatoly Bogachev. Despite his Russian heritage, he was raised in the Brighton Beach portion of Brooklyn and has no discernable trace of his motherland accent.

He wastes no time on pleasantries when I answer the phone. "Have you found her?"

Even though I'd located her three days ago, I lie. "Just today."

"And?" he prompts.

"She's in a small town called Cranberry, north of Pittsburgh." I don't offer anything more.

Anatoly is silent for a few moments, but his next words catch me by surprise. "Take her out."

"Take her out?" I repeat.

"Yes, yes," he exclaims impatiently. "Eliminate her."

"When?"

"Now," he snaps. "Get it done and return to New York."

I grit my teeth. Sometimes, he's like an overgrown child, despite the fact that we're both thirty-five. "I need time to plan this so it's done cleanly with no blowback on me and, more importantly, on you. I'll need to watch her for a bit to get to know her patterns. Figure how I'm going to do it. Where to dispose of her."

"Throw her in the fucking Allegheny River for all I care," he growls. I can just envision him in his office right now, pacing back and forth in front of his desk, fists clenched and desperate for me to carry out his dirty work. I've come to know him well in the past two years.

I take in a breath before slowly letting it out. "I'm your man, Anatoly. I can do this, but you've got to give me the time to be clean about it. I'm not going to fucking prison over some chick who broke your heart, whom you now want offed."

Anatoly snarls. "Watch it, Griffin."

At my peril, I ignore his warning. Anatoly Bogachev is extremely volatile and dangerous. "I need at least a few weeks. She's not going anywhere. I'm watching her closely. Once I have her all figured out, I'll be able to take her out in the way that best protects us all."

"Fine," he mutters. "You have two weeks."

"Thank you," I reply softly, knowing he prefers to be

addressed reverently to soothe his ego.

"And she didn't break my heart," he adds gruffly. "But she's a dangerous liability, which is all you need to know."

"I'll handle it," I assure him.

His reply is a quick disconnect of the phone.

The countdown starts.

♦

LEANING AGAINST THE headboard of my hotel bed, I cross my hands over my stomach and ponder. It's not hard to put things together. Anatoly wants Bebe Grimshaw dead. She got sent to prison for a thirty-five-year stretch around eight years ago for a crime, and she'd refused to name her co-conspirators. She's now free long before she'd be eligible for parole, and I've yet to figure out how she accomplished that.

Anatoly knows she's out of prison earlier than should be possible, and he doesn't want her to have an attack of conscience.

But why is she in western Pennsylvania when her roots are in Ohio?

I think about her actions over the last few days of tailing her. I rode my Harley down from New York because the weather was gorgeous for the end of September, but I've since rented a car. The pipes on my Harley are far too loud to be inconspicuous.

One thing I've noticed is how wary Bebe is. It's obvious by how she's always scanning her surroundings when she's out and about. She takes different routes into the city when she goes to work, and she carries a gun in her purse. Through her windows, I've watched her take it out in the evenings before she goes to bed. She carries it upstairs long after her mom and son have gone to bed, and I imagine she puts it under her pillow or by her nightstand.

She's scared of someone coming after her.

I'm betting that someone is Anatoly.

But still… how the fuck did she get out of prison? Her crime was serious. Yet, here she is, living a free life before paying her dues.

And what in the hell does she do for a living?

That first day I followed her into the city, I was shocked when she drove deeper into the seedier part until she'd finally pulled into an underground parking deck of an abandoned warehouse.

Except… it wasn't abandoned. There was a box near the rolling steel gate she'd peered into, which I'm sure it scanned her eyes. If that's the case, she's once again involved with some high-tech shit. Possibly another hacker group?

Anatoly runs a criminal syndicate loosely known as Kobaloi. His family backing is the Russian mob, but over the years—because he's smart as fuck—he moved more into black-hat crime. It's a means of hacking individuals and organizations for monetary profit. It's far more lucrative than mob work, which basically squeezes lessers to funnel riches up the food chain and launder money. I'm one of a handful of hired muscle he uses for any job he can think of, but mainly for protection.

Mob politics are extremely dangerous, and there are plenty of people who hate Anatoly.

My mind returns to that warehouse. I nab my laptop, which is next to me on the mattress, and boot it up. Google is my friend, and I start to navigate its murky waters of information.

It takes me about an hour of deep diving and testing hunches before I'm able to find out who probably owns the building. It's buried under three layers of corporate ownership, but I eventually come up with the name Joslyn Meyers.

Of course, everyone who's anyone knows who she is. She's an incredibly talented actress and singer who boasts multiple awards. I suppose there could be an argument that the warehouse is actually a secret recording studio or something, but I immediately dismiss the idea. No way it would be protected with security that involves a retinal scan. Music isn't that valuable.

I dive back into Google to read more news articles. A few more queries reveal Joslyn Meyers is now married to a man named Kynan McGrath, and there's a wealth of information about him. British, former Royal Marine, and current owner of Jameson Force Security—a huge private contract security company. Looks like it originated in Vegas, and it's now headquartered in Pittsburgh. The website is sleek, but it's too vague to give me the answers I need. Some well-worded crap about high-end security services, but the lack of true information makes me believe what they do is very much under the radar. Most likely contract work doing stuff for our government that it just can't do because of political constraint.

Regardless, this makes a bit more sense. Presumably, Bebe now hacks for the good guys. At least that's my guess given her skill level. Let's face it, she's no dummy if she was able to hack American nuclear codes.

That means she's probably more protected than I originally thought. I get why she's wary, too.

I'm relieved Anatoly gave me two weeks. This isn't something I can rush into.

I put the laptop aside, then lace my hands together behind my head. Staring at the ceiling, I consider the few places Bebe visited over the past few days—to and from work, to the grocery store, and to her son's school to pick him up. Each day after school, she takes him to the park to toss a football. It's sweet to watch them together. The kid is clearly her world now.

As far as I can tell, it's my only entry point to get closer to her.

The kid, I mean.

I decide to hit up the park tomorrow afternoon to figure out how close I can get to them.

CHAPTER 2

Bebe

"**A**ARON," I CALL from the kitchen, but I angle my voice toward the entryway into the hall which will hopefully carry up the stairs. "Let's go. We're going to be late for school."

"You need to install an intercom system," my mom suggests from where she sits at the kitchen table with a cup of tea.

"I'm not paying money to have an intercom system installed," I grumble. "Not when I have a perfectly good set of vocal cords."

"He plays music in his room." Picking up her cup, she looks at me over the rim, as if that makes what she says more authoritative. "He can't hear you."

"Aaron," I yell louder. My mom winces. Shrugging, I shove the turkey sandwich I'd made for my son into a plastic baggie and toss it in his lunch box. At the ripe old age of ten, he insisted he could no longer carry a superhero lunch box to school and requested a plain black insulated bag from LL Bean. My child is growing up. I missed way too much of his childhood, having spent the superhero years in prison.

Turning to the fridge to grab an apple to throw in, I ask my mom, "And you're sure you don't need me to take you to the doctor?"

"I'm totally fine," she replies with a dismissive wave before taking a delicate sip of tea. "Besides... it's just a routine visit."

It might just be a regular doctor's appointment, but I've missed a lot of years with my mom, too. While I was serving my sentence in a high-security prison in Fort Worth, Texas, my mom struggled to raise Aaron for me while battling diabetes in its worse form. She couldn't work and it took her years to qualify for social security, during which she and Aaron both suffered from not having enough money to do much more than subsist.

"Okay," I say, but then I give her my own pointed look. "If you change your mind, you just need to call me. I'll need about forty-five minutes lead time, but I can get back to take you."

"Stop fussing," she says with a stern expression, but there's a great deal of affection in her voice. She understands I need to do this for a while. I feel like I have so much to compensate for, even though my mother has never once blamed me for the mess I landed myself in or for the disadvantage it cast upon my son.

She's always loved me unconditionally. It's made all

the difference in my ability to integrate into a somewhat normal life.

"Fine," I drawl, smiling cheekily. "I'll stop fussing." But then I take a deep breath and bellow, "Aaron… come on. We're late."

"He can't hear you," she says again with a sage look of wisdom. "He's listening to his music."

With a sigh of frustration, I toss the apple in his lunch bag and stomp out of the kitchen while grumbling, "Never should have bought a house this size anyway. We only need half this much space. He'd be able to hear me then."

But as I make my way up the staircase, I know that given the choice to buy this house or a smaller one, I would have gone with this one. I wanted Aaron and my mom to have a nice place to live, especially given the hell I'd put them through. I needed to compensate for being gone for seven long years. When I'd been sentenced to prison, Aaron was three years old. I'll never know how hard it was for him because I couldn't bear to consider it. My mother diligently brought him out to visit me in Texas as much as she could, but money was tight so it wasn't often enough. It was usually managed through the generosity of family members who pooled their funds so my mom and son could make the long drive out there from Ohio. Beyond that, I had to make do with phone calls to try to develop whatever type of relationship I could with my son in that capacity. Once he'd started reading and writing, we'd communicated through letters, but that had been a horrible way to have a mother-son relationship.

I'm lucky though. My son is the most amazing kid in the entire world. He's bright and wise beyond his years, but he's empathetic to the terrible situation I'd placed myself in.

Yes, it'd been beyond reprehensible I got involved in black-hat hacking to begin with. I shouldn't have turned to crime to help make ends meet while struggling as a new mom, a college dropout, while also trying to help take care of a sick mother at the same time.

But then I was in too deep. The things they asked me to do became more complex, which meant the risk was way too great. When I tried to back away, I was reminded all too clearly I was going nowhere. I belonged to them forever. The insurance policy they had to make me stay and be a good little hacker was my son, Aaron. The threat was laid out all nice and clean… I was to do as I was told or Aaron would die.

It was that simple.

The only way I could get myself out of the situation was to get caught. I was tasked with hacking our government's complex framework to steal nuclear codes. It was the hack of all hacks, and I made myself into a legend while simultaneously dooming my life. I was not about to let our nuclear codes get away from me. I couldn't—in good conscience—put people's lives at risk like that. Besides… I love my country.

So, I intentionally got caught. My hope was if I went to prison, I'd at least be out of the clutches of the organization I worked for while Aaron and my mom would be free of my sins.

I should have been destroyed when I was handed a thirty-five-year prison sentence, but I couldn't be. The relief I'd felt over not having to worry about Aaron's life being at risk anymore had been too great. It made it easy to do my time with a clean conscience.

Pausing after I make my way to the top of the staircase, I glance over the railing at the living room. I bought new furniture and pretty artwork before we moved in, wanting to make this a real home for Aaron. It's crazy that just six months ago, I was in prison and receiving a surprise visit from Kynan McGrath.

Oh, the ego he had, striding into that meeting room to offer me a job. I thought he was fucking nuts, but damn if I didn't walk out of the prison with him that day.

A free woman and an official employee of Jameson Force Security.

The power Kynan commands with the U.S. government is slightly terrifying. I suppose he's done so much great work for them that he can pretty much name any price. In my instance, he wanted one of the best hackers in the world to work for him, which is how I'm now free and living in a four-hundred-thousand-dollar house I never could have afforded—not even in my wildest dreams—without having met Kynan McGrath.

Needless to say, Jameson pays me extremely well for my talents, which are now white and pure as snow.

I move down the short catwalk to the hall, which branches off. The master suite, which is mine, is to the right. Aaron and my mom's rooms, along with a bonus room over the two-car garage, are to the left.

I knock on Aaron's door, waiting for him to answer. Music blares on the other side, but he somehow hears me. In just a moment, the door swings open to reveal a cheerily smiling Aaron, his backpack slung over his shoulder.

He looks nothing like his father, who I can barely recall an image of. I got pregnant with Aaron my sophomore year of college while at MIT, and his father hadn't stuck around even to the second trimester. I tried to keep him updated as best I could after Aaron was born, but he wasn't interested in being a dad.

When I got sent to prison, I was terrified his dad would try to come back into the picture, but no... he was happy with my mom having full custody. Even though my heart bleeds over Aaron not having a father who's interested in him, I'm glad he's all mine.

Well, me and my mom's. She's as much his parent as I am, I suppose.

"Hey, kiddo," I say, reaching out to tousle his hair. "We need to work out a better system than me yelling up the stairs for you to get a move on and you not hearing me."

"What do you suggest?" he asks, his eyes dancing.

"Perhaps turn your music down, keep your door open, and your ears on high alert for any important messages from your old mom," I say sternly.

He just snickers and leans in—yes, he's as tall as I am—to kiss my cheek. "Sure thing, Mom."

I completely melt because first... he's a ten-year-old boy, so I'd expect legitimate sass. At least an eye roll. Hell, I wronged him so horribly by getting sent away to prison. It'd be completely understandable if he disobeyed me and blamed it on his shaky upbringing.

But my kid doesn't do that. He responds in such an affectionate, easygoing way that I sometimes think he's the real adult and I'm the child in this relationship. Aaron is such a love bug... he's the one who ends up treating me with kid gloves because he hates I've also suffered.

He moves past me to bound down the steps. I catch up with him in the kitchen just as he's bending to kiss his grandma on the cheek as well. I should be jealous of their tight relationship, but I can't be. I'm far too grateful they had each other to lean on in the years I was away. The bond between them was essential to their survival.

"What do you two feel like for dinner tonight?" I ask as I move to the coffee pot to fill up my travel mug. Aaron plops at the table, then starts wolfing down a quick bowl of cereal.

"I can handle dinner," my mom says as she stands, nabbing her teacup.

I automatically reach for it. "I'll make you another cup."

My mom ambles over, her flowered housecoat worn and well-loved. She moves right into me, puts a hand to my face, and says, "Stop trying to do everything, Bebe. You have nothing to prove."

God, she's so wrong about that. I have so much to prove, especially that I deserve this second chance at life. I need to be the best mom and daughter, and the best employee for Kynan.

But now is not the time to argue, because we are late. Smiling, I step around her to grab my purse. "Come on, Aaron. We've got to go."

He packs one more huge bite of cereal in his mouth before grabbing the box of Captain Crunch, intent on taking it with us. I'm okay with that, especially because he's still hungry. Smiling, he dips to give my mom a goodbye kiss.

"Think we can hit the park today?" Aaron asks as we head through the mudroom into the garage.

I wince because it's hard to get out of work early enough to take him to the park. I'd have to leave no later than four. While Kynan wouldn't care because I work from home as well—most evenings after everyone goes to bed, actually—I'd still feel guilty about it.

But not as guilty as I'd feel about not taking Aaron. He's trying out for a recreation football league next week, so he needs as much opportunity as he can to practice.

I'm not good at helping him. He wants to be a quarterback, and he needs someone to throw to. My job is to catch the ball, which I am only able to do about twenty percent of the time. The other eighty I'm running to retrieve it as it bounces away from me. But then I return it and let him toss me another. I'm basically a ball-return girl, but hey… it's what he wants. Besides, I owe him all the time in the world.

"Sure thing, kiddo," I say with a smile, waiting for him to precede me out the door. He moves around to get into the passenger side of my little Hyundai crossover. "I'll be home around four-thirty or so. Make sure your homework is done, then we'll hit the park for about an hour before dinner. Sound good?"

"Sounds like you're the best, Mom," he replies. Again, I'm hit with a sweeping wave of love for my child that is so deep, I wonder how in the hell I deserve the

"Smart-ass," he replies affectionately before disappearing into the elevator.

"What's he buying?" I ask. Already chewing the bite I couldn't resist taking, I move over to a stool at the counter to finish eating and to enjoy another cup of coffee before I start my workday.

"A briefcase," she replies, tapping her stylus to the screen. "And he chose the most hideous design, too."

Chuckling, I consider getting up from my perch to see the damage, but then I'm sidetracked by the sound of a door opening and closing.

The fourth floor, in addition to housing the kitchen and living areas, also has five personal apartments for any employees that are looking for a housing perk. The only ones currently taking advantage are Cage Murdock and Merrit Gables, both of whom relocated here from the Vegas office. It's Cage who appears in the kitchen from the hallway.

"Morning," he says tersely, heading for the coffee pot. Anna and I offer greetings back.

"What's on your agenda this week?" I ask.

Cage tenses slightly, his gaze moving over to Anna as he answers. "Heading to Al Hasakah tomorrow, so I'm packing today."

Anna doesn't even lift her head, which says this isn't news to her. Cage flicks his gaze to me. "We have a lead."

Finally, Anna gives a wan smile at Cage as she rises

from the stool, tucking her iPad under her arm. "You'll be careful?"

"Always," he assures her, his voice almost reverent.

Speculatively, I watch Anna move over to Cage. He bends readily to accept her hug. It's a tight one, Anna squeezing around his neck as he pats her on the back.

When she releases him, she turns to me. "See you around, Bebe."

"Later," I say.

Cage is at the kitchen island, halfway through one of three cinnamon rolls he piled on his plate. When Anna disappears into the elevator, I pointedly study him. He must feel the weight of my gaze because he finally looks my way. "What?"

"Do you and Anna have something going on?" I ask.

I don't need him to speak to get my answer. His horrified expression tells me I read that wrong. "God, no. What the hell, Bebe? She's just a friend. Practically a family member, really, just like everyone here. She just lost her husband, and—"

I hold my hands up. "I'm sorry for asking. Don't get so defensive. It's not like there would be anything wrong with it if it were true."

"Well, we don't," he reiterates sharply before returning to his breakfast. His voice drops slightly. "But... we have become good friends. I think she's just extra grateful I'm going back."

"Back" would be to Syria. I knew we'd had some leads on finding Malik Fournier. He's our teammate who has been missing since the FUBAR mission that killed Anna's husband, Jimmy, and one of our other members, Sal Mezzina.

"You going by yourself?" I ask as he digs into his second roll.

He shakes his head. "Small team. We're going in black as the government wouldn't sanction us."

He means this is black ops and off the books. "Why aren't we getting government support?"

Cage chews his roll. After he swallows, he wipes his mouth with a paper towel. "It's not just that we aren't getting support, but we've also been told we can't go in to look for him."

I blink in surprise. We do a lot of work for the government. We're one of, if not *the*, most trusted of their contractors. "But why not?"

He shrugs. "No clue. Probably because it's such a political mess over there. They don't want to risk any more U.S. citizens."

I scoff, the noise rumbling and deep. "As if we'd leave him behind. Surely they realize that."

"Oh, I'm sure they do. But none of us give a shit what the government says. We're not leaving Malik behind."

Amen to that. "Well, you've got the full support of

us back here. Dozer and I will have a close eye on you."

"Of course you will," he replies with a grin.

God, I hope he finds Malik. We have no clue at this point if he's alive or dead, but even if he's dead, we can't leave him behind. At least Anna got to bury Jimmy and Sal's family got to say their goodbyes when their bodies were brought back.

"She seems to be doing well," I muse. I pick up my coffee to take a sip, my thoughts returning to the young mother who lost so much so early.

"Anna's strong," Cage replies, and there's no hiding the hint of pride in his voice. They must indeed be close for him to feel that way, but I take his word there's nothing romantic between them. I tend to believe him as Cage isn't the settling-down type, but he's one of those guys who could have a good friendship with a female for sure.

I nod, deciding to switch the subject. It feels too much like gossiping, and that's just not me. My general curiosity has been appeased.

"I need you to stop by R&D sometime today. I've got some new satellite phones I can send with you. The GPS tech in it is off the hook. I can follow you in real-time regardless if the phone is on or off, and with new satellite relay, there won't be reporting delay."

"Sure thing," he replies.

We finish our breakfast in silence, then I head back

to the elevator. Our new Research and Development division is housed in the sub-basement level, and Kynan has spent a ton of money to give Dozer and me our dream facility. It officially opened last month. I love hiding down there trying to figure out better ways to communicate with and protect our guys. It's what I would have been doing with my life—had I stayed the course at MIT and not ruined my entire life over the prospect of easy money.

There's no solace in knowing the extra money was not for me, but to take care of Aaron and my mom. The fact is I turned my life to shit by choosing the wrong path.

The only thing I can do now is try to be the best at what I do for my coworkers and my family, while hoping it's enough to earn me some type of redemption before I die.

CHAPTER 3

Bebe

AARON'S GOING TO be tall like his dad, but everything else about him is all me, even down to the way he frowns. His combination of blue-black hair and pale blue eyes means I'm going to be beating the girls back soon.

Or maybe it will be boys.

Don't know, don't care, as long as he's healthy and happy. Of course I want him to fall in love, but not any time soon. For now, I'm happy being one of two strong loves in his life.

Whether it's due to his age or the fact he's happy to have me solidly back in his life, Aaron doesn't mind spontaneous acts of affection from me. So I loop my arm over his shoulders as we saunter over to one of the grassy areas of the park not currently occupied by other people. It's the last week of September and the first full week of fall, but the grass is lush and green. It's still incredibly warm in the western Pennsylvania area and today it's in the mid-eighties. I know we'll treasure this weather for as long as we can take it.

"How was school today?" I ask.

"It was good," he replies casually, never one to roll his eyes at my invasive questions or act too old to indulge his mom about her curiosities. People always remark what a great kid Aaron is, but then immediately warn me puberty will change that at some point.

I don't necessarily believe that. Maybe I'm being naive, but I also believe parenthood is an adventure. Coming from a place just six months ago where I never thought I'd have hands-on experience in raising my kid, I'm relishing every upcoming change.

"Grandma is cooking spaghetti tonight," I say, which is our favorite meal my mom makes. We'll eat until we're sick and groaning from the discomfort.

I stop walking, having reached a spacious spot of grass. Aaron doesn't hesitate, just keeps going. We've tossed the football plenty over the last few weeks, and it's our routine. He does glance over his shoulder with a grin. "Bet I can eat more than you."

I know he can, but I take the bet. "Five dollars."

"You're on," he calls before trotting a few feet away from me.

Aaron turns, positions his fingers around the laces, and cocks the football. I spread my legs a little, preparing for its flight into my arms.

It sails toward me, and I have to run a few feet to the

left to make the catch. Of course, I am the most unathletic person in the world, so it falls through my hands. I was nowhere even close to catching the damn thing. It hits the ground, tumbles away from me and I run after it like an idiot as Aaron laughs.

I bend, grab the football, and turn quickly to fling it back to Aaron. Of course, it barely covers the distance he just threw it and comes up too short for him to catch. Easily scooping it from the ground, he continues jogging up to me.

"Okay, Mom… you have to hold it like this before you throw it," he explains, then I get a lesson on proper throwing technique. He's explained it to me on no less than four other occasions, but I listen attentively, hoping to glean new information that will make me a little bit better. He hands the ball to me, then starts to trot backward. "Now… try it again."

I place my hand as he instructed and cock my arm back, but, before I can throw, movement to my left catches my eye.

Glancing at a park bench situated just adjacent to a cement pathway running alongside the grassy area, I have to restrain myself from my jaw dropping. Plopping down with a book in hand is perhaps one of the best-looking men I've ever seen in my life.

I mean… he's probably not for every woman, but he totally pushes my buttons. For one thing, he's big. For some reason, despite my tiny size, I've always loved an intimidating size. He's tall and built with thickly muscled arms that are tattooed all the way down, encased under a tight black t-shirt. His long hair is in a low ponytail at the nape of his neck. By the length, it's probably to his shoulders. Best of all, he's got a beard that's sweetly kept and trimmed and full, generous lips.

He stretches out his long legs, which are clad in faded jeans and sturdy biker boots and crosses them at the ankles. Leaning back, he starts reading a thick paperback, which makes him even more attractive.

"Mom," Aaron calls. "Throw the ball."

I shake my head, my face flushing, when the man's head starts to raise in response to Aaron's voice. Spinning toward my son, I disregard everything he just taught me and fling the ball so hard I almost throw my shoulder out.

Aaron starts laughing as it sails over his head, then takes off running after it. I refuse to turn back to the gorgeous, biker-looking dude while hoping to hell his book is more interesting than my horribly awkward attempt to play football with my kid.

I mentally kick myself for caring about something like that. A cute—okay, phenomenally gorgeous—man is of no significance to me. I've been given a new lease on life, so my focus and energy must go toward Aaron and my mom. It's the only way I can be remotely deserving of this second chance.

Except, a little voice in the back of my head whispers, *you deserve something for yourself, too.*

I squash it, because it's not true. I don't deserve anything more than the beauty of my family, which I've thankfully been returned to.

Aaron nabs the ball from the ground, cuts a few feet to the left, and notches his arm back. He lets it go, just a little to my right this time, which forces me to chase it. I move for it, determined not to let it hit the ground again. Sadly, I'm a day late and a dollar short. I come nowhere close to making the catch. When it thuds against the turf, it does a wonky bounce and tumbles end over end, right toward the man.

"Shit," I mutter. Watching in horror, I realize the man has been watching us when he easily bends to scoop the ball up with one hand before it bounces off his kick-ass, steel-toed boot.

As I reluctantly walk toward him to retrieve the ball, he puts his book down and stands. Up close, he's way taller than I thought, towering more than a foot above me. His eyes—and wow, they're green—are sparkling with amusement. He only spares me a glance before he turns to Aaron and gracefully launches the ball. It hits Aaron square in the chest in the most perfect of passes.

"Sorry about that," I murmur, but my words fall on deaf ears. To my disgruntlement, Aaron is overjoyed at having someone who can actually get him the ball. Without even asking if it's okay or worrying about infringing on the man's time, Aaron lobs it right back to him.

Smiling as he makes the easy catch, the man calls. "Loosen your grip up slightly. It will help your spiral."

"Okay," Aaron replies eagerly, waiting for the man to throw the ball back.

I stand there, completely ignored, as this stranger intrudes upon my time with my son—while doing much better than I ever could.

I silently seethe, even though I try to be charmed that's he's helping my son. He's even giving him good advice about technique, which is something I could never do.

"I'm Griffin, by the way," the man says in a deep, rumbly voice, sounding as if he's amused by me.

He peruses me with his lips curved upward.

"I can give you some lessons, too," he suggests. And damn it… I ignore the tremor moving up my spine at that unintended, completely innocent, yet somehow suggestive offer.

"Um… no thank you," I mutter.

Griffin shrugs, but he continues tossing the ball with my kid.

"Got a name?" he asks after a particularly spectacular pass.

I jolt at the request, the wariness I'd forgotten to have over the last ten minutes or so rushing over me. I don't talk to strangers. I'm not interested in men or dating or anything that requires polishing off my trust-building skills.

Still, I find myself answering. "Bebe."

"That's an interesting name," he remarks. "And what about your kid?"

"Aaron," I reply, but he promptly ignores me to yell new instructions. "Now, Aaron, I want you to run deep a few paces, cut left, and really take off."

"Got it," my son calls enthusiastically. I watch in amazement as he sort of jukes an invisible opponent, cuts left, and takes off on those gangly legs of his. When he looks over his shoulder, he's easily able to catch the ball. Aaron shouts with glee, spikes the ball into the ground, and does a dance resembling the funky chicken.

I bust out laughing, my head tipped back and my hands going to my belly.

Griffin shifts my way, and I shiver when he says, "That's a beautiful laugh."

I sober instantly. "Are you flirting with me?"

"Apparently very poorly if you have to ask," he replies with a wink.

And damn it... I *am* charmed. I'm also equally pissed because it makes me want to talk to him. Shooting him a glare I don't really mean, I petulantly ask, "So what...

are you like a football star or something who just hangs in parks and waits until a woman comes along to showcase your skills?"

Griffin laughs, and it's deep, booming, and infectious. I can't help but smile.

"Now that's funny," he says with good humor. "And to answer your question, I played football in high school and was okay at it. And on a whim, I took my bike out today because the weather is fabulous. I came to the park to read a little."

Bike?

I scan the parking lot on the other side of the path, spotting a sexy Harley Davidson in a flat black.

Damn it. Another button pushed.

"Well, thank you for taking the time to give Aaron some instruction," I feel compelled to say. "He's trying out for the rec team soon, and I don't have the skills you do to help him. So this has been great."

"Sure," he replies easily. Aaron tosses him the ball, and I get unduly sidetracked by the muscles flexing in his arm as he catches it.

Griffin regards me with an earnestly hopeful expression. "Would you let me take you and Aaron out for an ice cream after we finish tossing the ball?"

My entire body flushes with mortification when I realize I'm being asked on a date. Sure, he's included Aaron, but I can tell by his appraising eyes it's really about me.

I love and hate it at the same time, because I haven't been asked out in over ten years. For seven of those years, I was in prison. The three prior, I was busy being a mom and a master criminal.

"Actually, my mom's cooking dinner. We have to be going soon to make it." Then I decide to turn him off, thinking it's the best way to shut him down. "We live with my mom, actually."

His expression softens. "That's cool. I love my mom to death, and I wished I lived closer to her."

Damn it.

"Here's another suggestion," he continues. "How about you let your mom feed Aaron tonight, and I'll take you out to dinner."

Okay, perhaps what he'd offered before wasn't actually a date, but this most certainly would be.

"Um… well," I stammer. "It's um… spaghetti night. My mom's gone to a lot of work, and it's my favorite."

He hesitates before giving a slight nod of understanding. "I can see that would be important. And you don't know me well enough to invite me to your house for a home-cooked meal, so how about you let me take you to dinner tomorrow night?"

Gah… why does he have to be so charming on top of fantastically gorgeous? "Um… you see… the problem with that is—"

"Hey," Aaron exclaims as he comes barreling toward us. My face burns with the knowledge we've been soundly ignoring him. "Are you going to throw the ball again?"

Griffin smiles at my kid, sticking his hand out to shake. "I'm Griffin, by the way. You've got some natural talent, kid."

"Thanks," Aaron replies with a deep blush. He shakes Griffin's hand like a man, and I realize my kid just grew up a little on me.

I use this moment to make our break. "Honey… you need to thank Griffin—"

"It's Griff, actually," he butts in. "My friends all call me Griff."

I ignore the pointed remark, which says he very much wants to be my friend, but I'm betting in ways that aren't rooted in friendship. I hate it makes butterflies zoom in my belly.

Inclining my head in acknowledgment, I turn my attention to Aaron. "Thank Griff for helping you out, but we really need to head home. Grandma will be expecting us soon for dinner."

"Thanks, Griff," Aaron says with a big grin. "That was awesome."

"Be glad to help you anytime, kid."

"Tomorrow?" Aaron blurts out.

"No… wait," I exclaim, realizing if I don't shut this

down, this man will stay in our life. I truly don't want that.

"Sure," Griff replies, sliding a well-intentioned smirk my way. "How about ten AM? Your mom can sit her pretty butt on that bench over there and read a book. I'll toss the ball around with you for a while."

Oh no, you don't buddy. I'm not about to have you force me into something I don't want.

"Grandma can bring you since I have to work," I tell Aaron, which isn't true, but I'm not going to let Griff one-up me. Shooting a simpering smile at Griff, I say, "I'm sure you two will have a great time without me, and my mom loves to watch Aaron play."

Challenge flashes in Griff's eyes, and my belly gets the butterfly zoomies again.

Griff leans slightly toward my son. "I know your mom is probably not going to like this, because she's doing her best to resist me, but I happen to have three tickets to the Steelers game on Sunday afternoon. Would you and your mom like to come with me?"

My eyes widen at his audacity, even as I vaguely hear Aaron hooting and hollering over this offer, jumping up and down like a mad man with excitement. Griff gives me a triumphant look.

"That was low," I hiss, but I can't hold back the tiny smile threatening to break free. That was well played, and I could never deny my son the opportunity to see a professional football game. He hasn't been to one before, and he's adopted the Steelers as his favorite team now that we've moved here permanently.

"We'll meet you at the stadium," I say, cutting off any attempt he might make to try to pick us up.

"Fair enough," Griff says, then tosses the ball to Aaron. Giving him a soft clap on his shoulder, Griff bends to look him in the eye. "You did really great today. I'll show you some new stuff tomorrow, okay?"

"Yeah," Aaron blurts out, his eyes sparkling with glee. "That would be great, Griff."

Griff gives him one last smile before shooting me a wink. "See you Sunday, Bebe."

I glare at him. Inside, though, I might admit to smiling a tiny bit.

CHAPTER 4

Griffin

A TTENDING A PROFESSIONAL football game at Heinz Field is definitely an experience I won't regret. I'm a Bills' fan myself, but I've always had great respect for the Steelers. While the game has been great, it's been even better watching a ten-year-old who can't contain his excitement. Aaron repetitively jumps up and down in his seat, once prompting someone a few rows back to yell for him to sit down. I turned in that general direction, eyes scanning for the fuckwad who would steal a little kid's joy and leveled a murderous glare around at the people. No one said another word after that.

The clock ticks down the last few seconds of the half, and a horn blares to call the end of the play. I reach into my wallet, pull out forty bucks, and hand it to Aaron, who is sitting in between Bebe and me. "Go grab us some food and drinks, kid."

Aaron snatches the money, then starts to push past his mom. Grabbing him by the collar of his shirt, I give him a playful tug. "Hey… see what your mom wants first."

Aaron gives me a sheepish grin, then looks down at her. "What do you want?"

"Hot dog," she replies. "And a diet coke."

"Sure thing." Aaron starts to move past his mom. As an afterthought, he glances over his shoulder. "What do you want, Griff?"

"Same. And get whatever you want, obviously."

"Thanks," he calls before darting into the aisle, thrilled at the freedom to be on a mission on his own inside Heinz Field.

Bebe's gaze follows him as he moves with the crowd up the cement stairs leading to the main concourse where the food stalls are located. I move over, plopping into the seat Aaron had vacated as his placement there was clearly strategic. It made it hard to talk to her during the game, so I figure I've got a good fifteen to twenty minutes while Aaron is getting food.

"Having a good time?" I ask.

She casts one last, "worried mother" glance at Aaron before bringing her eyes to mine. Her smile is genuine. "Of course I am, but, more importantly… Aaron's having the time of his life. I really can't thank you enough."

"He's a good kid," I say truthfully. I like being as honest as I can, when I can, and no doubt… her son is a pleasure to be around. "And he has some talent."

CODE NAME: HACKER

"Really?" she asks hopefully, her expression going soft and wistful. "He's nervous about tryouts."

"He'll be fine," I assure her. Her gaze doesn't linger. It drops to her lap where she twists her fingers with agitation.

I make her jumpy… I can tell.

"So, what is it you do for a living, Bebe?" I ask to get her talking. I need to figure out as much as I can about her, and the clock is ticking down on Anatoly's demand.

She freezes, her eyes darting to me in what I think is panic, but then her features smooth out just as quickly. "I'm in IT."

"Computers, huh?" I give her an encouraging smile so she'll continue. I would love to find out what she does inside that abandoned warehouse.

"More like low-level computer repair," she replies with a jittery laugh. "Just a strip mall computer store, you know?"

No, I don't know, Bebe. That's a definite lie because I know you don't work in a strip mall.

"How about you?" she asks.

My lie comes more easily since I've given it some thought. I need to be as non-threatening as I can. "I'm a lineman for the power company. Just relocated to Cranberry about a month ago."

"Why Cranberry?" she asks. While I'd like the attention to be on her instead of me, I know the easiest way to

41

get her to open up is to make her comfortable.

"I'm originally from upstate New York," I say, another truth. Always best to keep it as real as possible. "My parents had a small dairy farm. Not really a city guy. I figured Cranberry was close enough to the Burgh for my work needs, but it still gives me that country feeling."

"I know exactly what you mean," she murmurs.

"So, is Aaron's dad not in the picture?" I've been genuinely curious about this. I couldn't find anything in the news articles I'd read, but there were hardly any mentions of Bebe having a kid, either. Guess that wasn't newsworthy compared to the crimes she was charged with.

Bebe shakes her head. "Never has been. Just been me, and well… my mom has done so much for Aaron. For both of us."

Yeah… raised your kid for seven years while you were in prison.

And even as the thought comes to mind, I realize I don't have an ounce of negative judgment for Bebe. What little bit I've come to know and observe, I almost feel sympathetic to whatever it is she was doing. I have no idea what drives people to commit the crimes they do, but, in Bebe's instance, I almost have the feeling she was probably naively lured into a bad situation.

Now, I have no proof. Maybe that's why what is left

of my conscience is telling me to give her the benefit of the doubt.

Not that it will make a difference in how this will turn out, but still… there's something about her that deeply intrigues me, well beyond the information I need to collect per Anatoly's request.

"For what it's worth," I say sincerely, "I think you've done a great job raising that boy on your own."

Again, her gaze drops to her lap. "My mom helped a great deal."

"Still." I pause, forcing her to look at me. "He's a good kid who clearly adores his mother. That means something."

Bebe blushes, scanning the field that's empty except for the media personnel on the sidelines.

"I'm wondering what it's going to take to get you to go out to dinner with me." Once again, her eyes snap to mine. Her mouth parts, a tiny gasp escaping as if she's completely shocked by my request.

I have to wonder just how naïve she is, because I've learned she's not a dummy. Bebe is incredibly smart, so any confusion on her part must be because she's been out of the dating game for so long.

I press my advantage. "Come on, Bebe. Put me out of my misery. I'd love if you'd accept a simple dinner invitation."

"But… but… I don't even know your last name."

"Stoltz," I say. Another lie.

"But—"

"Just say yes," I encourage in a low voice. "If you don't want me to pick you up at your house, we can agree to meet at a restaurant."

"But," she says again, so I shore up my resolve to keep the pressure up. However, she immediately backpedals. "Wait… you know what," she breathes heavily, giving what appears to be a self-chastising shake of her head. Her eyes meet mine, clear and determined. "Yes… I'll have dinner with you. But I would like to meet you at the restaurant."

"Tomorrow night?" I don't want to give her any time to change her mind.

"Sure," she replies. "I just have to make sure Aaron's set up for the night and has his homework done. But I can meet you any time after seven."

I lean in toward her, giving her shoulder a playful bump with mine. "Now that makes me very happy indeed, Bebe 'I-don't-even-know-your-last-name'."

Also a lie. I know it well.

She laughs. "Grimshaw. It's Bebe Grimshaw."

Grinning, I tease. "Going to tell me what Bebe stands for?"

"Not until I see how much I like you after the first date." Her eyes dance with playfulness.

♦

WHEN ANATOLY GAVE me two weeks to handle his problem, I made quick work of renting a furnished apartment in Cranberry. I certainly had no clue at the time whether I'd need the cover, but it was a good preemptive move.

It's a small one-bedroom, and it came fully furnished. While I have no plans or even hopes Bebe will ever come here, I can explain the lack of personal mementos as having just moved here and have yet to unpack or something.

For now, it's just as comfortable as the hotel I'd been staying in, and Anatoly never balks at my expenditures. While he may be grumbling because I asked for extra time to complete his task, he knows I've always been trustworthy and I don't ask for unnecessary things. If Bebe decides to check me out—and let's face it, she has the abilities—I want to make sure I appear legit.

I unlock my new apartment door, balancing a bag of groceries under one arm. After the football game, I said goodbye to Aaron and Bebe after programming her number into my phone and promising to call to arrange our dinner date. I then set off on some errands, which included not only the grocery store, but also the car rental agency to extend my lease for another two weeks on the off chance I need to surreptitiously follow Bebe again. She's already seen my bike.

Finally, I went to the mall and splurged on some

nicer clothes for dinner tomorrow night. While I get the distinct impression Bebe doesn't care about trappings like that, I feel like I should try in case I'm wrong. Nicer clothes for me mean jeans that aren't so faded and threadbare as well as a black button-up shirt versus my standard t-shirt or Henley I normally wear for comfort.

I move into the apartment, locking the door behind me. After I take a moment to unload my groceries, I head into the small living room.

Deciding to preempt the inevitable call that should be coming soon, I call Anatoly to update him. It always soothes his anxiety when I provide him information before he asks.

He answers on the second ring. "Talk to me, Griff."

"Spent some time with Bebe Grimshaw this afternoon," I say.

"You actually talked to her?" he asks incredulously. "Or you killed her?"

"Talked to her," I clarify, ignoring his grunt of disappointment.

"And what did you learn?"

"Not a lot just yet. She's a little closed off. I'm having dinner with her tomorrow."

Anatoly barks a laugh. "Dinner? Are you fucking kidding me?"

"Relax," I say in a low voice. "You want to learn whatever you can, this is the way to do it."

"Can't believe you're fucking dating the target," he mutters petulantly. "I don't want this to drag on."

I roll my eyes. Despite being the kingpin in a massive criminal enterprise, Anatoly can act like a child at times. "Just hang tight. She's settled into a new life here. She's not going anywhere. From what I can tell, she's working a very nondescript job in a strip mall. My gut says she's flying way under the radar, and she just wants to live a peaceful life."

Not sure why I feel the need to say that or why I blatantly lied about where she works. I know nothing I can say will ever assure Anatoly enough to call off my mission.

"She's feeling secure in her life," I say. Another lie, but I'm adept at making them up when needed. "She's not looking over her shoulder. Kind of just keeps her head down, goes to work, and comes home."

"What about her kid?" Anatoly asks, and I jolt. "I remember she had a kid, right?"

I have to be careful I don't reveal the entirety of the information I'd found researching Bebe. Anatoly tells me what I need to know, and he expects me to do what he asks without further question.

I play stupid. "I haven't seen a kid yet. She hasn't mentioned one. I'll find out, though."

"You do that," he replies, and there's no mistaking his sinister tone. I expect if he wants Aaron dead for some reason, he'll ask me to take care of it, too.

For now, though, he merely says, "Keep me updated."

Anatoly disconnects the call, and I lean back into my couch cushions with a sigh. This is definitely getting more complicated than I had originally considered.

CHAPTER 5

Bebe

THE RESEARCH AND Development division at Jameson Force Security is sort of what I'd envisioned for my career back when I was an undergraduate at MIT and before I got lured to the dark forces of black-hat hacking. To work in a lab with the smartest minds, developing the most miraculous of inventions, and watching them be used for the forces of good.

Yes, I am in my dream career right now. Just as I often don't believe I'm fortunate enough to have my son back, I often wonder how I got to be so lucky to land this.

Currently, I'm working on an artificial intelligence module that can help guide and predict outcomes based on patterns we put in. We're tweaking the speech synthesis, so our AI—who we've weirdly named Bob— can recognize unlabeled words and phrases, as well as categorize them. Bob, therefore, can listen in on our meetings as we plan and develop missions, make hypotheses, and render opinions on outcomes.

Of course, it's still in the early days and we'd never trust Bob in making any decisions, but we've been testing his theories against our own. So far, he's a pretty smart dude.

The motion-sensored sliding glass door swishes open, and Dozer walks through. When I said I envisioned working with the brightest, Dozer fits that description. He has an IQ of 170, and Kynan stole him from NASA. Dozer is one of those types who knows something about everything. Lately, I've been referring to him as Tony Stark, but, frankly, he's far better looking than the guy behind the Iron Man mask.

I'd think a former NASA scientist would be sporting pocket protectors and thick-rimmed glasses, but Dozer looks like a cross between a flashy sports celebrity and fashion runway model. He's got sharp cheekbones, exotically tilted eyes, a perfectly proportioned nose and lips, and the body of a Greek god.

The smart hottie has something in his hand that makes him infinitely more attractive. He walks over to my desk—which is more of an elevated worktable—and hands me a Starbucks venti salted-caramel mocha.

I release an exaggerated moan as I take the cup. "You are a god."

"Yes, this I know," he says, flashing me a brilliant grin that sparkles in contrast to his midnight skin.

There was a time when Dozer and I shared a kiss.

It was a drunk kiss one night after the whole team had gone out. We'd had way too much to drink, and he was new to the team and lonely, I think.

I was lonely as hell, too, not having had any male companionship in years.

Unfortunately, drunk kissing is the worst kind because the reasons behind it aren't clear. Was it true attraction?

For me, it was attraction. I mean… the man is as close to an Adonis as possible.

Or was the alcohol the real troublemaker, removing inhibitions that might have a damn good reason for being there? I mean, workplace romances are never a good thing.

Ultimately, it was bad timing.

Turns out, I was lonely, but I wasn't ready to let the solitude go. I wasn't ready to open myself up. Dozer said a similar thing to me the next morning at work when we awkwardly laughed about it. He had merely said he'd been through a tough breakup and just wasn't ready for anything.

Since then, our friendship has continued to grow and flourish. He's the closest thing I have to a best friend in my life.

"Have you started exporting yesterday's tags?" Dozer asks as he moves over to his computer. He also has a standing worktable adjacent to mine with the same three flat screens I have so we can monitor multiple sources of information.

"It's downloading now," I say before taking a delightful sip of my coffee.

"Hey," he says as he turns to face me. "Can I ask you for a personal favor?"

"Sure," I reply easily, holding up the coffee cup in a silent toast.

"Think I can leave Brutus with you next weekend? I'm going out of town."

Brutus is Dozer's tiny little Yorkie dog that Aaron and I have dog sat on occasion.

"No problem," I say. That's not even a favor, and I can't help but tease. "Got a hot date?"

"Actually, yeah," he replies with a cheesy smile before turning back to his computer screens.

This is not unusual. Dozer dates lots of women, and I asked him about it once following our kiss that went nowhere, especially since he had told me he wasn't ready for anything.

"These are hookups, Bebe," he'd told me. "Nothing serious. What you and I could have had… that would have been serious, and I'm not ready for serious."

So Dozer has become one of the resident playboy studs of Jameson. He and Cage should start a tally competition to see who can bang the most women.

I'm not sure why thinking of Dozer's noncommitment type of love life prompts me to say something, but I end up blurting out, "I had a date last night."

Dozer freezes and slowly pivots to face me, his mouth hanging open. It's no secret I've been averse to dating. Everyone under God's green earth has tried to set me up on dates over these last few months at Jameson, and I shot them all down.

"I met him in the park," I continue, feeling the need to have Dozer like Griff. "He played football with Aaron. He's blue-collar. Like salt-of-the-earth kind of guy, you know? And he took us to the Steelers game on Sunday, and well… I had dinner with him last night."

Dozer's mouth sags even further, then he drawls exaggeratedly, "Ho-l-y-y-y-y sh-i-i-i-i-t."

He moves over to me, presses an arm onto my work-table, and leans closer. "This is epic. Tell me everything."

I don't want this to be epic. Epic scares me so I start to backpedal some. "I mean… he's not that great. Nice guy, sure. But I'm not looking for anything—"

Dozer's hand comes out and covers my mouth, stopping me in mid-backpedal. He shakes his head, giving me a chastising smile. "No… tell me everything. Don't waste time with excuses about why this is a bad idea, but tell me all the good stuff."

I blink and he stares back, conveying a threat within his gaze… if I don't give him what he wants, he's going to put his hand back over my mouth. I know how stubborn Dozer can be. He'll hound me relentlessly until I divulge all.

When I sigh, he takes that as my capitulation and removes his hand.

"His name is Griffin Stoltz. And he's from upstate New York, recently relocated here to the area. He works for the power company, and he's great with Aaron. Doesn't seem freaked out I have a ten-year-old kid. And well…"

I think about Griff and how amazing he looked last night at dinner. We'd met at a small Italian restaurant for dinner. He had on a pair of dark jeans and a button-up shirt that fit him well. His hair wasn't pulled back, but he'd left it loose and wavy down to his shoulders. With his shirtsleeves rolled up to mid-forearm, showcasing tattoos and muscles, there's no getting past the fact I'm incredibly attracted to him. My body and mind have not reacted to a male like this in years, and it sort of wigs me out.

"Where'd you go?" Dozer asks, snapping his fingers in front of my face. When I shake myself out of it, I find him grinning. "You got a real dreamy expression on your face just now. Remembering the hot after-date sex you had with him?"

My hand automatically flies out to slap him in the chest. "God, no. I just met the guy."

"So?"

I roll my eyes. "So, I'm not the type to just jump into bed with someone."

"Well, you should be," Dozer asserts with a wink. "I mean… as long as you're safe about it, why not? It's the twenty-first-fucking-century, Bebe. Everyone has sex and hookups."

Is this true? Have I missed a new sexual revolution, or perhaps it was already there but I was too busy to notice?

I mean… I have a good gut feeling about Griff. He seems down to earth and easygoing. I ran a background check on him after I acquired his last name at the football game, and he's got nothing more nefarious on his record than a parking ticket.

Our dinner didn't last long since I had to be up early this morning to make it in to work for a meeting with Kynan. The hour we'd spent together dining on shared plates of gnocchi and bruschetta was spent mostly talking about the things we both liked and had in common.

That would be seventies' classic rock, the Sopranos, and hiking. I'd spent a good chunk of the summer hiking local trails with Aaron, and I shared those spots with Griff as he meticulously typed them into the Notes app on his phone.

Toward the end of dinner, I was glad it was ending, if only for the fact I knew we'd venture into more personal information before too long, which meant I was going to have to lie to Griff. I wasn't about to tell him I'd spent the last seven years in prison because I didn't want to scare him off. My hope was I could skirt that little tidbit with some redirection and deflection, but the bottom line is... I like him well enough to risk that awkwardness to see where this goes.

I simply can't ignore the fact that he's the first man to even spark my interest in more than a decade.

As Griff walked me to my car, he asked me out again. More specifically, tonight, and I accepted. He'd leaned in and my breath caught in my chest, thinking he was going to kiss me, but all he did was brush his lips against my cheek before murmuring, "I had a really nice time, Bebe. Looking forward to tomorrow night."

"Bebe," Dozer chides with a low chuckle. "Lost you again."

"Sorry," I mutter, swiveling toward my workstation. "Was just thinking about the date last night."

He returns to his desk, but he feels compelled to remind me, "That didn't end in hot sex."

"Nor will it," I say primly.

"Prude."

"I am so not a prude," I insist, spinning toward him. "It's just... isn't sex only supposed to come after like date five or something?"

Dozer snickers, turning to fully face me again. "Bebe... I love you dearly, but you need to jump back into life with both feet. You've missed out on so much, and now you're just hiding. But you've taken a step forward by going out with this guy. Now, I'm going to give you some important advice."

Leaning toward him, I listen with keen ears. I trust him implicitly, so I'm going to listen.

Dozer takes a step toward me, then puts his hands on my shoulders. He ducks his head so he can stare me in the eyes. "You sacrificed your life to protect those you love and your country. You paid a price. Now you need to get your ass out there and live life to the fullest. If you want to wait until date five to have sex, you do that. But if you want to bang his brains out before your second date even starts, you do that, too. Both are the right answers. In other words, you do what makes you happy."

Could it really be that simple?

That I should stop worrying so much about appearances and norms, and just do what makes me happy? My gaze drops to the floor as I ponder this, but then pops up to lock with Dozer's. "But I'm scared. I mean, what if this doesn't go anywhere? How do I even begin to explain my past to him? How do I build something with someone when I don't even know if my past is going to catch up with me in a really horrible way?"

"All legit worries," he replies softly, giving my shoulders a squeeze. "But you can't let them hold you back. As for how much you share with this guy, I'm going to tell you to trust your gut. One thing I've learned about you over the last several months is that you have a great gut instinct. Don't share if it doesn't feel right. If it does feel right, know it's a risk to divulge this and be prepared for the worst. I mean... what's the worst that can happen? That he decides he doesn't want to see you anymore?"

I nod glumly. That would suck. I've often regretted my poor choices, but never once had those regrets been focused on me. I've always been worried about how everything affected Aaron or my mom. Now I see there's a longer-reaching impact. My crimes are always going to follow me.

"Then may I suggest," Dozer advises with dramatic flourish. "That you fuck him first before you tell him so you can at least have a little fun before he dumps your ass."

I can't stop the hoarse bark of laughter, and I let it lead me right into a quick hug. Dozer holds me tight for a second, gives me a squeeze, then releases me.

I have no clue what's going to happen tonight, but Dozer's advice has opened up a hell of a lot more possibilities for me.

CHAPTER 6

Bebe

"**Y**OU SURE THIS is cool?" Griff asks as we walk into the biker bar.

I nod, and the reason it's cool is because Griff had taken a hold of my hand after we'd exited my vehicle. It's amazing how the simple touch of a man's hand against mine can cause the butterflies to zoom around my belly again. It reminds me of my first real boyfriend in ninth grade, and I can remember how glorious it felt the first time we walked the school halls while holding hands.

I'd taken Dozer's advice to stop worrying so much. I'd even relented and allowed Griff to pick me up at my house, but honestly… that was more the fact I'd run a background check on him that turned up clean.

He'd rumbled up my driveway on the Harley, but after he'd come inside, met my mom, and said hello to Aaron, we decided to take my car since rain was in the forecast later that evening.

We went out for dinner first, and I found it oddly comforting he suggested we eat at TGI Fridays. It wasn't fancy, and I appreciated the low-key atmosphere. We both sat at the bar, ate ribs, and drank a beer while we chatted.

Again, it was easy talk. Favorite movies, favorite foods, favorite books. After dinner and as we were waiting for the bill, Griff said, "I'm not ready for the evening to end yet. How do you feel about playing some pool or something?"

I'd loved the suggestion because I wasn't ready for it to be over either. Every passing minute, every little thing I learned about this man, made me like him just a little bit more.

The biker bar he chose is one he'd been to before. He didn't make attempts to assure me that he's not a bar fly or he didn't drink excessively. I like he's confident enough he doesn't have to explain how he knows about this bar.

Griff grabs us a beer, and we find an empty table near the back. It's not overly crowded as it's still early—barely eight-thirty—and a Wednesday night to boot.

Griff teases me as he racks the balls. "Are you a shark? Should we lay some money on this?"

Chuckling, I tell him the ugly truth. "I haven't played pool since college, and that was a long damn time ago."

His head pops up, eyebrows rising. "College, huh? Where did you go?"

Shit. That information is too close to my eventual downfall. Still, I answer with a breezy smile. "MIT."

Griff's mouth hangs open slightly. "Damn... I didn't realize you're a genuine brainiac. What was your degree in?"

I laugh nervously, playing it off as best I can. "Not too much of a brainiac. I dropped out after my sophomore year. Pregnant with Aaron."

He nods in what appears to be understanding. I'd left the implication heavy in the air that my pregnancy caused me to leave college when, in reality, it was the fact I'd gotten way too deep into cybercrime.

"I admire you raising Aaron on your own. Getting pregnant in college couldn't have been easy."

"Yeah," I reply a little thickly, shifting away from his gaze to grab a pool stick off the rack on the wall. "Thanks."

When I turn around, Griff has finished racking the balls and stands at the high-top table we'd set our beers on. He doesn't mention the pregnancy or Aaron again, for which I should be grateful, but he ends up asking about something even worse.

"So, tell me more about your job," he says.

I internally wince, knowing the questions are just going to get more personal. I'm nowhere near ready to tell him about my horrible truth. Dozer told me to trust my gut on when the right time would be, and I can affirmatively state now is not that time.

I move over to the table, take a long pull off my beer, and set it down. "Oh, it's not all that interesting. I basically do minor computer repair, software installation, and troubleshooting for customers."

"Is that what you were studying at MIT? Computers?"

"Yeah," I murmur, my gaze dropping to my beer bottle. I have a moment of sadness over what could have been had I stayed on the righteous path. "Guess that stuff sort of comes naturally to me."

"Well, dairy farming came naturally to me," he says with a booming laugh, "but I didn't like it at all. So the moral to that story is just because you're good at something doesn't mean you should be doing it for your career."

"I'll drink to that." I chuckle, picking up my beer bottle and tapping it against his. "But seriously… dairy farming can't be all that bad."

And just like that, Griff is off and running, explaining about his family's farm in New York and just how backbreaking the work can truly be. I'm relieved because the attention has been taken from me and the potential avalanche of lies I'd have to keep telling him the more he asked. For the time being, I'm happy to listen to him talk.

Over the next hour, we sip at our beers, play pool,

and flirt. Either I'm not as rusty at flirting as I thought I'd be, or the beer is making it easier, but regardless, it's fun.

I'm having a good time, and I can't remember the last time I just enjoyed myself with another human being.

Griff smiles a lot. When I try to scoot past him to line up for a shot, he'll move out of the way just enough so he has to touch my hip or my arm as I move by. There's a tiny thrill each time it happens.

And there's laughter.

I've had so little to laugh about for so long—because, let's face it, prison isn't a happy place—that my face actually starts to hurt. But Griff is funny and self-deprecating, and I'm hopelessly drawn to him as the night wears on and the beers keep coming.

Another couple saunters over and asks if we want to play doubles, and Griff and I agree. They're not local, just visiting some family and out for a night of fun away from the kids. We have a great time with laughter and more beers. At some point, I end up leaning into Griff and his hand comes around my waist as we watch our opponent take a shot on the pool table. I feel protected. Despite the fact it's not an overly intimate touch, I feel desired.

I can feel it radiate from him, which makes Dozer's words reverberate through my head about how I should go for it.

Around eleven, the other couple leaves and Griff and I finish our last beer.

"Listen," he says, taking my hand. His green eyes are mesmerizing. "I've had way too much alcohol to drive you home. I'll pay for a cab for you."

My head tilts in question. "What will you do?"

"I live within walking distance. Just a few blocks from here."

"Hmmm," I murmur, glancing at the pool table. I'm sad our evening is ending because this has all felt new and magical. I never thought I'd have this again in my life.

"Or…" Griff says, which causes me to snap my head his way, my eyes locking on him. My pulse speeds up. "You could come to my place. I'll make us some coffee."

"I'm not ready to have sex with you," I blurt out, but then immediately cringe. "Oh, my God… I have no clue why I just said that."

"I didn't have any expectation we'd have sex," he says with a chiding smile. "Truly… just coffee. But I'm also glad to get you a cab."

"I'm not averse to sex in general," I say. Once again, I sort of shrink backward with a full-body cringe. "Oh God… why did I say that?"

Chuckling, Griff steps into me and puts his hands on my hips. "Just relax, Bebe. We aren't going to do anything you don't want to."

"I'm just so nervous all of a sudden," I babble, continuing in a rush of tangled words. "And my friend Dozer told me to not get wrapped up in my head about this and to do whatever I wanted to do, as long as I'm safe, and well... I do feel safe with you and we'd have to be safe about sex, so I guess that—"

Griff's mouth comes down on mine, effectively shutting me up, and I start to sink into oblivion. His kiss is so fantastically amazing, and I lose myself in it. After another few moments, I know if he told me to get naked and get on the pool table, I'd do it. It has to be a combination of alcohol and forced celibacy, but the deeper part of my psyche realizes Griff has the power to make me feel so much more if I ever gave him a shot.

Way too quickly, his mouth is gone and he's smiling down at me. "Let's go to my apartment. We'll have some coffee and sober up so cooler heads prevail, but I'm still going to need to put you in a cab at some point. It's a work night for us both, and we won't be safely sober enough to drive for a while. So let's just go hang for a bit longer. We can plan our next date."

"There's going to be another date?" I ask curiously, my lips still tingling from his kiss. My chest constricts from the sweetness of his words.

"After that first kiss?" he asks with a wink. "You're damn straight there's going to be another date."

When I laugh, it comes from a genuine place within me that I haven't opened up to many other people. A part I thought might have died from living in isolation and fear for seven years. But it feels good. Besides, the way Griff's eyes light up from the sound makes it even better.

We leave the bar, hand in hand, and walk the few blocks to Griffin's apartment. It's small, but clean and nicely furnished. "Sorry it's a little bare," he explains as we enter. "I've still got all my stuff in storage from the move."

"I can help you unpack sometime if you want," I offer, glancing around the living room.

Griff moves into the kitchen, then starts the first cup of coffee in his Keurig. "Sure, that would be great."

There's not much to see in his apartment. There's a short hall off the living area that has two doors—presumably, a bathroom and a bedroom. I move into the small kitchen just as the first cup of coffee is done brewing.

Griff hands me the cup, then points to the fridge. "Cream is in there. Hope you don't want sugar as I don't have any."

"Black is fine," I reply, giving a tiny huff over the steamy top before taking a sip. While I like my frothy cappuccinos and sweet confections in my java, years of only having black coffee available in prison made me adaptable.

Griff rests a hip against the counter as his cup brews, pushing his hands into the front pockets of his well-fitted jeans. "When are Aaron's football tryouts?"

"Saturday." I mimic his stance, leaning against his counter with my coffee in hand. "He's so nervous."

"I can practice with him some more if you want," he offers.

"Really?" It's the sweetest offer, because Aaron is anxious about it. "We don't want to be a bother."

"You and Aaron are not a bother," Griff chides with a stern frown. "And he's a good kid. I enjoy helping him out."

"He really appreciates what you taught him. I have no skills whatsoever. Without a male figure in the picture, it can be challenging with a boy."

Griff nods, his eyes sympathetic. "I can only imagine."

"So you had a close relationship with your dad?" I surmise.

"Very," Griff says with a chuckle. "I mean... a lot of time was spent working on the farm with him, which isn't always the most fun, but he's a good listener... my dad. I can talk to him about anything. And he taught me how to throw a football and how to fish."

"See, I worry I'm not able to give everything Aaron needs—"

"You give him exactly what he needs," Griff interrupts. "You may not know what the hell you're doing with a football, but you were out at the park with him, encouraging him to play. That's all that really matters to a kid, Bebe."

I look down at my cup, sadness starting to fill me. "I wasn't always the best mom. Wasn't always available to him."

I risk a peek at Griff, wondering if this is the time to spill my guts about my history. He gives a slight shrug. "No one is perfect, Bebe, but what I do know is your kid seems happy and well adjusted. I'd say you've been a damn good mom to him."

And right there... I know I can't say anything because Griff is already giving me too much credit. He's built me into someone I'm not, and I'm not ready to see the disappointment on his face when he learns about the real me.

Maybe I should just do as Dozer says. Fuck him and have fun. This doesn't have to be anything more than a casual hookup that can help me to scratch an itch that's been brewing for a long damn time.

I put my coffee cup down, not wanting to do anything to interfere with my buzz and the courage it's giving me to take a step toward the sexy man across from me.

CHAPTER 7

Griffin

SOMETHING COMES OVER Bebe. I can see it on her face. While I may not have known her long, I've come to read her very well. She has deep secrets, and I think she's struggling to keep them contained. I've honestly been waiting all night for her to tell me about her time in prison. I figured the four beers she had would help loosen her tongue, but she's kept it all close to the vest.

And now... her expression morphs from what seemed like a bit of sad nostalgia to something a little predatory and challenging.

She places her cup on the counter, then takes a step toward me that puts us toe to toe. I have no clue what's coming, but I have an inkling I should ignore my own coffee, which has finished brewing.

Bebe's head tips back, and she looks so magical right now. All waif-like and innocent, those crystal blue eyes blinking with her well-guarded secrets stashed behind the veil. Her hands come to my chest, and my muscles leap at her touch. I wish I were immune to her, but I'm not. I very much want her to keep doing whatever it is she's wanting to.

"I think I'd like you to kiss me again," she whispers, her eyes locked straight on to mine. Her voice is strong and sure. While she may not be willing to reveal her secrets, she's clearly offering something else.

Her lips are soft and inviting. The short kiss we had in the bar was all too fucking good. I wasn't brought to Cranberry to kiss this woman or play football with her son, but fuck if I can withstand the invitation she presents right now.

My hand goes to the back of her neck and she actually sags slightly, silently submitting to me. In this moment, she's placed her trust in me. She has faith I will give her what she needs, and I won't hurt her in the process.

She stares unblinkingly, her mouth slightly parted to give me the access I need.

If Anatoly were standing here right now, he'd remark how easy it would be to just tighten my hand around her neck. I could easily strangle her one-handed because she's so fairy-like, but two would get the job done quicker. She'd never be able to withstand my size and strength. I could put her down quickly and quietly, giving Anatoly whatever peace he thinks only her death can bring.

From there, it would be easy enough to get her in the

trunk of the rental in the black of the night. Drive eleven miles west to the Ohio River, attach a few cement blocks to her body, and toss her over a bridge.

It would be the best move. Giving Anatoly what he wants keeps me safe. If I fail to ultimately deliver her death to him, it will assuredly mean my death. He has no room for error, mistakes, or disloyalty. I could effectively end it all right now and stay on my boss's good side, which means I continue to lead a healthy life.

Except that doesn't seem to matter that much to me in this moment, with Bebe all soft and pliant before me.

I dip my head as I squeeze the nape of her neck, bringing my mouth to hers. Her breath flutters over my tongue, and she gives a tiny, almost imperceptible moan that almost drives me to my knees. Bebe is so hungry for intimate contact, and I can feel her practically vibrating.

Her fingers tighten into my shirt, and she tries to tug me closer. I place my free hand on her lower back, pulling her in tight. She gasps, feeling my erection, which started forming the minute she asked me to kiss her.

When I slide my tongue into her mouth, her response is a groan so guttural she sounds like she's in pain. But it's not really something that hurts. It might just be that the pleasure causes such overwhelming sensations it could be considered painful.

Regardless, her response is like a punch to the gut,

and my kiss turns more invasive. Bebe doesn't shrink away, but rather it feels like she's trying to meld with me as her tongue duels alongside mine. Her arms move around my neck, her tiny body plastering against mine. She feels way too fucking good.

Tearing her lips free of mine, Bebe glances up with a pleading expression. "I need…"

She averts her eyes, and I move my hand from the back of her neck to her chin. I force her to give me her attention. "What do you need?"

I don't get a response at first, but then a long-suffering sigh comes out. "I need to be touched. It's been so long, Griff."

She has no idea I know how long it's been—assuming she's not been with anyone since she got out of prison six months ago. And while I don't owe her a damn thing, I feel like my only goal in life is to give her exactly what she needs.

"Hold tight," I rumble just before I kiss her again. I briefly feel her mouth move into a smile against mine, then I have her tongue again.

I waste no time. Gliding my fingers down the side of her neck, I ever so lightly continue over her chest and along the side of her breast. She presses into me, but I let my hand drift lower, over her stomach and to the button of her jeans. It pops open easily, and her breath catches as I lower the zipper.

Pausing, I pull my lips away and stare down. She has her eyes squeezed shut, a pained expression on her face.

"Are you sure?" I ask. Her eyes flutter until she's staring at me with so much earnest anticipation, I feel absolutely unworthy of her.

She nods, her teeth sinking into her lower lip. She's not intentionally trying to be sexy, but fuck if my cock doesn't start thumping in response.

Her hands press into my shoulders, and she goes to her tiptoes in an attempt to reengage our stellar fucking kiss. My fingers inch into the waistband of her panties, over her smooth stomach, and down into the dark recesses below. Bebe jerks as my fingers brush through her soft curls, right into her wetness.

She growls, the sound so deep and needy I can only respond by pressing a single finger deep into her. Bebe jerks, cries out, and pulls her mouth away from mine only to bury her face into my chest. She writhes against me. For a moment, I do nothing but let her ride my finger, fascinated by the need driving her body to react. I've never seen anything like it. It's fucking beautiful.

I withdraw my finger and circle her clit. Bebe whimpers into my chest. With my other hand, I grip the hair at the back of her head and pull her back so I can see that gorgeous face.

"Look at me," I order. Her eyes pop open, hazy at first, but then they focus. "Let me have those eyes while I make you come, yeah?"

She nods mutely. I continue sliding my finger against her, circling, pressing, massaging. I hold her by the hair, forcing her to look me in the eyes. Within mere moments, I make her come hard. Bebe cries out my name, finally succumbing to the pleasure by squeezing her eyes shut and groaning out a brutal release. Her hips jerk, swivel, trying to draw out the pleasure, and I let her use my fingers a little longer because I want her to feel good.

Bebe gasps hard and when she finally gives me her regard once again, I can see realization start to set in that I just gave her an orgasm. She looks embarrassed... hopelessly lost.

Then her hands fly to my belt buckle, and she starts to work at it. Her gaze drops when she mumbles, "Let me give you—"

I clamp my hand down on hers. "Stop."

Her gaze jerks up, and she frowns in confusion. "But I want..."

"I know you do," I assure her gently, dipping my head down to press my lips briefly against hers. "But I somehow feel like this was important to you, and you don't owe me a damn thing."

"But I want—" she starts.

"I know," I murmur. "I know you do, but we have time to get there. Doesn't have to be tonight. How about we just cherish this moment, okay?"

I can see on her face that she doesn't understand. She's not sure if this is a rejection.

I do the best I can to reassure her. "Bebe... you are fantastic. And I can't wait to see you again. Tomorrow night if you'll let me, okay?"

Her lower lip trembles slightly, and she averts her eyes. Her voice quavers slightly. "That was amazing... what you just made me feel."

"I'll give it to you again, anytime you want," I say.

That gives her the courage to meet my eyes once again. The corners of her mouth tip up, and I get a sheepish half-smile. "Like I said... it's been a while."

"Yeah... you came pretty fast. It was spectacular."

Her cheeks turn rosy from the erotic compliment, and I have to wonder why I stopped her from opening my fly. Despite my restraint and caution, I've never wanted to fuck someone more in my entire life.

And yet... it's complicated.

Because I *should* be killing her for Anatoly right now.

♦

I STAND OUT on the street, watching the cab pull away with Bebe tucked safely inside. We suffered through a bit of awkwardness after Bebe came back down to earth, and I let my hard-on naturally subside. After I made us new cups of coffee, we sat at the kitchen table and talked about Aaron.

Oddly, after I'd used my fingers to make her orgasm, the safest thing to talk about seemed to be her son. Neither of us has to acknowledge we'd just taken a big step in intimacy with one another, and we weren't exactly sure what to do. I was sent here to eliminate Bebe. She's holding dark secrets from me.

Let's face it… we can't be any good for each other, right?

When the cab's taillights recede, I turn slowly for my building and trudge up the stairs rather than take the elevator. Once inside my apartment, I clean up the kitchen before heading to my bedroom. I feel a heaviness inside as I remove my clothes and slide under the covers.

My phone rings. Without even looking at the screen, deep in my gut, I know it's Anatoly. We haven't spoken in a few days, and he's someone who likes to stay up on everything.

"Hello," I answer as I connect the call.

"How about giving me a fucking update every once in a while, Griff?" he growls into the phone.

"Nothing to update," I say flatly. "She's been working and going home."

"When are you going to do it?" he asks.

"I've got a plan—"

"When?" he barks.

"This weekend," I say.

He goes silent. He's obviously trying to figure out something else to bitch about because Anatoly loves to be in control. He's the boss, and he leads by instilling fear and insecurity.

"Don't fuck this up," he finally says. "Because you will not like how I'll react if you do."

"I've got it under control," I assure him. "I've got a plan."

"Good," he replies. "That's really good. Call me when it's done. Better yet… send me photos. I want to see your handiwork."

I roll my eyes, something I take great pleasure in. "You got it."

Anatoly disconnects, and I toss my phone on the nightstand. Lacing my fingers behind my head, I stare into the darkness and try to imagine what a normal life would look like.

Could someone like Bebe ever be a part of it?

Most likely not, as I'm not a normal dude.

Regardless, I have some hard decisions to make, and they need to be made soon. I'm out of time with Anatoly, and I have a job to do.

CHAPTER 8

Bebe

"**B**ROUGHT YOU COFFEE," I chirp at Dozer as I walk over to his workstation.

I'm not a "chirpy" kind of person by nature, but I woke up feeling different. Maybe it was the flush of excitement over what might be budding between Griff and me, or maybe it was the fact I'd had the best orgasm of my entire life in his kitchen last night, but I chirp at Dozer.

He knows this is unusual, and his eyes narrow as he accepts the Americano with soymilk. "You're awfully chipper this morning."

"Chirpier," I quip back, turning to my workstation.

"Huh?"

I glance over my shoulder to see he's clearly confused. "Let's just say I had a date with Griff last night, and it went very, very well."

"Oh, I get it," he drawls with a cheesy grin. "You got laid."

"No," I correct with a schoolmarm look. "But I did

fool around, and it was awesome. He's awesome."

"Good for you," Dozer exclaims before giving his attention to his computer.

I'm smiling as I log onto my workstation. The retinal software I'd implemented to button up our security on this building has also been applied to each person's computer. The red beam of light slides over my eyeballs, and my unit starts to boot up.

An alarm emits from Dozier's computer, and I recognize the sound. If mine was fully booted, I'd be getting the same alarm. It's from our external security cameras that are mounted around our building. They are programmed with an algorithm to go off if any passersby show too much interest in our building—like if a person continually walks by, stops and studies the building for too long, or attempts to access the gated garage.

Dozer reacts quickly. By the time I move over to his station to hover over his shoulder, he's pulling up the camera feeds onto one of his large screens that sits atop the table.

I get dizzy as I zero in on the camera pointed right at a rolling steel gate that closes off our underground garage. Standing there staring directly at the camera... is Griff.

"Go get Kynan," I whisper to Dozer, not because I don't want to be overheard but because all the air has been sucked from my lungs.

"Who is that?" Dozer asks, not budging from his seat. On the video screen, we watch as Griff pulls his phone from his back pocket and starts tapping on the screen with his thumbs.

My cell phone chimes, indicating I have a text. It's clearly from Griff. I move to my desk, nab my phone from my purse, and pull up the text.

Let me in.

"Who is that?" Dozer repeats.

"Griff," I murmur, staring spellbound at his image on the screen. He leans up against the brick support column. Casually crossing his arms over his chest, he lets his gaze wander over the street.

"Why is he here?" Dozer asks as he moves off his stool and starts for the door.

"No clue," I reply, my ears now starting to ring with what I'm sure is an increase in blood pressure. "But please… just get Kynan quickly."

Dozer leaves, and I reply to Griff's text. *Just wait. I'm sending someone out.*

I watch on the screen as Griff reads my text, looks at the camera, and gives me a stiff nod. He does not appear to be a happy camper right now.

I don't feel like chirping anymore.

It takes less than a minute for Dozer to get Kynan, who then grabs Saint Bellinger, one of our agents, and meets Griffin at the steel gate. I watch this all on the video screen, moving from camera feed to camera feed.

I'm unfazed when Saint pulls a gun, leveling it on Griff while Kynan opens the gate. I'd expected this because the facility is pretty well hidden, and the fact Griff is here spells trouble. While the camera feed has no audio, Kynan clearly says something to Griff that puts him at ease enough to hold his arms out and stand still while Kynan moves in to pat him down.

Kynan finds no weapon, yet that does nothing to ease my anxiety. The two men exchange words with Griffin doing most of the talking.

Dozer appears back at my side, leaning in to stare at the men. Like me, I'm sure he's wondering what the fuck is going on.

"Did he know where you worked?" Dozer asks.

"He thinks I work at a computer store in a strip mall in Cranberry."

"Clearly, he doesn't think that," Dozer mutters.

Kynan pulls his phone out. He taps something on the screen, and it causes my phone to ring. He stares into the camera, waiting for me to answer. I do, eyes on the computer screen.

"I'm bringing him inside," Kynan says when I connect the call. "Get Cruce and Dozer, then meet us in the conference room."

♦

I STAND IN between Cruce and Dozer. They're tall and

solidly built, both dwarfing me. They have their arms crossed over their chests, glaring through the glass walls of the conference room. Kynan talks to Griffin as they stand tensely near one another. Can't hear what they're saying, but neither looks happy. Saint sits in one of the chairs, listening intently. He looks perplexed.

"I don't like him," Dozer says after a moment.

"That makes two of us," Cruce adds.

Both men are clearly being protective of me, but I can't help but stand in coalition with them. "I don't like him either."

Because the creepy motherfucker has managed to follow me to my place of work. For the life of me, I cannot fathom why.

Kynan twists his head, sees us standing in the hall, and motions us in. My feet feel like lead, but I make myself move.

I force myself to keep my eyes locked on Griff as I enter the conference room. He returns it, jaw set in iron and lips flattened in dismay. What the hell does he have to be so pissy about? It's *my* privacy he's violated.

It's tensely silent as Kynan moves to shut the door, then pulls the blinds on the floor-to-ceiling glass that looks out into the hallway.

Once we have absolute privacy from the rest of the company, I pivot toward Kynan. "Why is he here? Why did he follow me—"

Griff interrupts. "My name is Griffin Moore."

I turn in shock. "No. It's Griffin Stoltz."

"No, my last name is Moore. Stoltz is my alias. I'm undercover with the FBI."

"Bullshit," I mutter.

"I checked him out," Kynan offers. "Made a call while we were walking in here. He's legit."

My knees go weak. He's here investigating me? But I haven't done anything wrong. I work for a legitimate company, and I paid the price for my crimes.

Well, actually… I never paid the full price. Kynan got me released from prison well before I was eligible for parole.

A horrifying thought occurs to me. I grab Kynan by the arm, holding on desperately. "I cannot go back to prison, Kynan. It's not fair."

"Relax," he assures me, taking hold of my hand and giving it a squeeze. He nods over to Griff. "He's not here for you."

I spin back to face Griffin. He looks neither apologetic nor friendly, but with Kynan holding my hand, I feel secure. "What do you want?"

"Anatoly Bogachev," he replies, and those two words cause bile to flood my throat. I choke. Kynan's hand tightens on mine, and his arm comes around my waist to support me. This doesn't escape Griff's attention, and his eyes narrow on Kynan.

"I see you know who I'm talking about," Griff says curtly.

I nod. "Head of Kobaloi."

"Kobaloi?" Dozer asks.

Griff turns to answer his question directly. "I work in the Cyber Division of the FBI. Anatoly Bogachev is Russian mafia, and he's suspected of managing and directing a major cybercriminal enterprise that spans numerous countries. It's been called Kobaloi after a Greek monster that loved to trick mortals. I've been undercover for the past two years working for him, trying to get enough information to bust up the ring. He's the one who had Bebe steal the nuclear codes."

I can feel Kynan's hand jerk just as I can feel the weight of Cruce, Dozer, and Saint's stares on me. None of them knew who I worked for when I was arrested. Not one single fucking person in this world knows, because I refused to give up the information. I knew if I kept my mouth shut and took the fall, Aaron and my mother would stay safe.

It still doesn't explain why Griff is here. I pull my hand free from Kynan, move to the edge of the conference room table, and place my palms on it. Leaning toward him slightly, but glad for the distance and the solid table between us, I demand, "You seem to know a lot about me, but you lied to me, you asshole. What is your game?"

Kynan places his hand on my shoulder, but I shake it off, glaring at Griff.

He sighs, scraping his fingers through his hair. "I'm basically Anatoly's muscle. He sent me here to find you. I didn't know why at first. Had no clue what you were to him. After I located you, I googled you. Was able to piece enough together from the news articles about what you were arrested for to realize it was Anatoly you worked for. He somehow found out you got out of prison, and he ordered me to kill you."

"So you cozy up to me and my son to get the job done?" I screech. "You lied to me. Played me."

"I was trying to figure out what to do," he replies calmly. "I was trying to keep you safe while salvaging all the hard work I've done for two years to bring this fucker down."

"No," I snap, pointing an accusing finger. "You need my help to bring him down. What—now you think I'll just be your little government witness who will get up on the stand and testify against him for making me steal those nuclear codes? Well, you got another think—"

"That's not it," Griff barks. "I mean, yes… you have information, but I have so much more than what you could give me. I don't need you to make my case, Bebe. I'm on the verge of having enough to take this fucker down for the rest of his life, along with the other people involved. What you have is small potatoes. Frankly, I'm not fucking interested in it. The government already prosecuted that crime."

That effectively shuts me up, a stark reminder I was the actual criminal there, even if I was doing it at Anatoly's command.

I move over to Dozer to stand beside him. I'm so furious right now that Griff lied to me that I don't even know what to think.

"So you're here, insinuating yourself into Bebe's life, and you—the FBI—had no clue Anatoly was part of the nuclear-code crime Bebe got nabbed for?" Kynan asks.

"I put it together after I found out who Bebe is," Griff maintains with a curt nod. "But that's not why the FBI is investigating him."

"What exactly are you investigating him for?" Kynan asks.

"I can't tell you exact details," Griff maintains. "But the main case is for a ransomware scam."

Dozer snorts. "Seriously? Ransomware? You stalk Bebe and scare her half to death for a half-wit hacker who infects people's computers with ransomware?"

"He's stolen over a hundred million dollars from people," Griff replies tightly. "It's not a light crime."

"Holy shit." Kynan whistles low. "That's a lot of money."

"He's the highest priority in the Cyber division right now," Griff asserts. "And I cannot let this thing with

Bebe get in the way."

"This thing with Bebe?" Cruce growls, taking a threatening step toward Griffin. Kynan holds an arm out, silently telling him to stand down. "You were hired to kill her. You lied to her. It's more than just a 'thing'. We can't trust you."

"Except I'm here now—blowing my cover—telling you the truth," Griff grits out through his teeth, clearly getting fed up. "Bebe's life is in danger. Anatoly wants her dead. If I don't deliver, someone else will come for her. And I have a huge case I've poured my heart and soul into—my fucking life for two years—and I need to salvage that at the same time."

"And just how do you suggest that happens?" Dozer asks.

Griff directs his attention to me, and for the first time, I see a bit of remorse there.

"We have to kill Bebe," he states.

CHAPTER 9

Griffin

"COME AGAIN?" KYNAN growls.

It's clear all the men in this room are super protective of Bebe, but Kynan's the one I need to watch out for. I've done enough research about him to know he holds powerful connections in Washington. He's also just as big as me, and I'm sure he wouldn't think twice about breaking my neck if he thought I was a true hazard to Bebe.

"I need Anatoly to think I carried out my mission," I clarify to the group. "So we need to fake her death. Enough to convince him that she's not a threat so I can return to my work in bringing him down."

"So you fake Bebe's death… then what?" Dozer asks.

My attention moves across the room to the man who had walked in with Bebe. He's been watching me with keen speculation. I have no fucking clue who this dude is. He's built like a linebacker, has the face of a runway model, and yet, within his eyes, I can tell he's intellectually superior to every person in this room, including

Bebe, who's pretty fucking smart.

"Then I can go back to New York where he's located. My entire case stems around his business dealings there. The whole point of me going undercover was to get close to him, and I'm as close as anyone."

"And just what am I supposed to do?" Bebe asks, her voice a tad shrill. "I mean… once you kill me off, just what the fuck am I supposed to do? Because I clearly can't lead my normal life when I'm dead."

"You're going to have to go into hiding," I say gently. "Until we can arrest him."

"Oh, fuck you," she yells, something akin to hatred blazing in her eyes. "I was a prisoner for seven years. Do you think it's acceptable to take away my freedom again?"

Nobody answers her. Anything I say won't seem logical or feasible to her. I get her anger.

"Does anyone think that's acceptable?" Bebe repeats, addressing the men in the room. When no one responds, she spins on me. "This is your fault. The minute the man asked you to kill me, you should have let us know. You should have arrested that slime bag for wanting to murder me. That's enough to bring him down. You should have taken him off the streets, so I don't have to lose my life again."

Kynan strides to the door and opens it. "Everyone but Griffin needs to get out."

No one moves a muscle.

"Out," he orders, motioning around the room before his gaze settles on Bebe. "I need to talk to him privately for a moment."

Bebe glares at Kynan, then pins those venomous eyes on me for a long moment. Finally, she huffs and stomps out of the room with the rest of the men following her. Kynan glances at me. "I'll be right back."

Then he leaves, too, shutting the door behind him.

With a sigh, I pull one of the high-backed leather chairs away from the conference table and settle into it. My elbows go to the armrests and I lean my head back, briefly closing my eyes.

This has turned into such a clusterfuck. My two years of hard work is circling the drain, and I need to plug it fast. Worst of all, I've not only scared Bebe terribly, but I've hurt her. I let the personal stuff go too far in my quest to learn as much as I could, yet in hindsight, I don't regret a single intimate moment with her.

Or her son for that matter.

Another time and another place, Bebe and Aaron would have fit nicely into my life. I like her a lot. Too fucking much, actually, but I can't let her be the priority right now. Taking Bogachev and his crime syndicate down is the most important thing to me.

The one thing Bebe is absolutely right about though,

is I owed her the truth a lot sooner than this morning. At the least, I owed it to her last night after she came on my hand with my name tearing free of her throat.

Fuck… that was sexy and fuck me to hell, I want it again, but I can't.

The conference room door opens, my eyelids pop up to see Kynan slide in.

I sit up straighter in my chair. He walks over and takes the chair next to me, turning it so we're facing each other. He leans back, propping an ankle over the opposite knee as he holds his cell phone loosely in his hand.

"I want to know everything about your mission against Bogachev because this has not only put Bebe in danger, but her family as well."

I shake my head. "I can't tell you. It's classified—"

Kynan holds his phone out. I glance at it, then back to him. "Your boss is on the line. You'll want to talk to him."

There's no stopping the blink of surprise or the way my jaw drops. I take the phone from him, put it to my ear, and tentatively ask, "Max?"

My boss, Max Valentine, runs the cyber division of the FBI. His voice is fatigued, and it's obvious he's not happy about this. "Share everything with him."

"But why?" I ask, my gaze moving over to a smirking Kynan.

"Because we've been stalled, and we could use their help," he says with a heavy sigh. "Because Bebe Grimshaw is one of the world's best hackers. Because we may need her testimony at some point on the nuclear-code scheme to bolster our case against Bogachev, and we need her on good terms with us."

This all makes sense. Yet… I don't want Bebe involved in this. Bogachev is incredibly dangerous, and I don't want to put her at further risk. Still, it's not my place to say these things, and I can guarantee Bebe doesn't care for my opinion on this.

"Understood," I grit out.

"You have the full authority of the government to get whatever inside information you can on Bogachev by utilizing any means necessary that Jameson can help you with. I'll put through the necessary documentation on it."

"I'll handle it," I assure him, not knowing what Jameson can actually do to help me. I still have to go back to New York to try to figure out a way to break into Bogachev's system to download the incriminating data to prove our case. Right now, the only things I have are the hundreds of criminal activities I've overheard him talk about. My testimony alone won't be enough.

I disconnect the call, then hand Kynan his phone.

"I need to know exactly what type of danger Bebe is in right now," Kynan says as he steeples his fingers under his chin. "Will Anatoly trust you when you tell him you killed her?"

It's a good question, and I give it to him straight. "I'm in deep with him, but Anatoly doesn't trust anyone. However, I think if I give him photos and some documentation, he'll accept my word on it. He's far too busy to doubt me unless he has reason to believe I'm lying. Right now, I don't know why he'd doubt me. I've never given him a reason to do so. All that being said, he's unpredictable. Some say he's batshit crazy. The one thing I know for sure is he's incredibly dangerous. While he's a twenty-first-century guy making his dirty money off cybercrime, his background is Russian mafia. He didn't think twice about ordering Bebe's death."

"What about Aaron and Gloria?" Kynan asks.

"I'm not sure," I say truthfully. "He asked me if there was a kid in the picture. He must have remembered Bebe had a child. I lied and told him I hadn't seen a kid. In fact, I didn't give him much info about Bebe. Never divulged exactly where I'd located her or what I'd seen."

"Thank fuck for that," Kynan mutters.

"I wasn't going to put her in unnecessary danger. Despite how you must feel about me, know that from the moment he sent me to Cranberry to look for a woman, I operated in a manner that would protect her from whatever Anatoly had planned. That was my sworn duty to the FBI."

"Even if it meant risking your cover?" Kynan asks skeptically.

"Yes," I simply affirm.

Kynan nods, his expression clearly grateful. "Now, tell me what you're doing to bring him down."

I push forward in my chair, moving to the edge and leaning a forearm on the table. "About five years ago, we got whiff of some hackers operating out of Ukraine and Russia who were targeting U.S. citizens, among other countries. We started tracing backward as best we could, but cybercrimes are incredibly hard to track to the source because of proxy servers and such. So we ended up using some CI's—"

"CI's?" Kynan asks.

"Confidential informants," I explain. "Low-level black hats. And the word on the street was Bogachev was behind a huge ransomware cyber heist."

"What's that?"

"Basically, we believe he orchestrated his hackers to send out an email to millions of people with a ransomware virus. It does as you'd expect… takes the computer hostage until money is sent in exchange for the code to unlock it. It's simple but effective. People depend on their computers."

"And people really fall for that?" Kynan asks incredulously.

"You'd be surprised. Mostly it's the elderly and other

naïve folks. He can effortlessly send out a hundred million emails. Let's say only five percent fall for it, and they pay one hundred dollars. That's five hundred million. As the money comes in, it's immediately sent out to virtually untraceable private offshore accounts."

Kynan whistles low. "Unbelievable. But you're not going after Bogachev for the nuclear-code scheme Bebe went down for?"

I shake my head. "That was not on our radar. Had no clue he was involved until I researched who Bebe was. That case had been essentially closed. Besides that… we were looking at a completely different type of crime. The ransomware that was deployed went to millions of people. The nuclear codes had a single Chinese buyer."

"So you're on to Bogachev now, and you go undercover," Kynan summarizes. "And you gain his trust somewhat, start to gather information—"

I nod. "My job is to try to hash his network."

"Hash?"

"Create a forensic image of the data we're seeking," I supply. "We've got warrants in place. So far, I've not been able to gain physical access."

"Can that information be gleaned remotely?"

I shrug. "Not by any of our people. We've tried, but his security systems are too advanced."

"Maybe Bebe can do it remotely," Kynan ponders. "What exactly do you have tying this to Bogachev besides informants?"

"Not a lot of hard evidence," I admit. "Mostly stuff I've seen and heard over the past two years. I'm pretty much his right-hand man when it comes to protection and carrying out odd jobs for him. I'm by his side at all meetings and phone calls. I drive him around and listen."

Kynan's lips flatten. "So you have nothing."

"I know where the information I need is physically located. At his New York apartment. He has a very secure office I've been inside many times, but never alone. It's protected by extreme measures. But if Bebe could hit him remotely..."

"We'll have to talk to her about it," Kynan muses. "You'll have to go over everything you know with her."

"Of course," I reply, ready to get on with this. Ready to get this shitstorm over with. "Let's do it."

Kynan holds his hand up, a grimace on his face. "She's really, really pissed at you. You're going to need to let her cool down a bit, but she'll get over it."

"Bebe doesn't seem the type to get over something very easily," I say.

Kynan chuckles. "She can totally hold a grudge, but she has a vested interest in bringing Bogachev down. She knows her life can't be normal again until he's behind bars. If I know her, she's on the computer right now trying to figure out how to hack him."

I nod, not liking the fact I'm going to have to work

with Bebe. She's too much of a distraction. I don't want to be her partner. I want to be her…

Well, I don't know exactly what I want, except a little bit more of what we had last night in my kitchen and a lot less of Anatoly Bogachev fucking with her life.

"I suggest you get out of here for now," Kynan remarks, dragging me from my dark thoughts. "I'm going to need to talk Bebe off the ledge right now. She's so pissed she probably has your real identity located and is currently draining your bank accounts."

No clue what the expression on my face is, but it makes Kynan laugh.

"Relax," he says, slapping his palm on the table and standing. I follow suit. "Let me go talk to her. Be here tomorrow morning at eight. We'll start planning what to do about faking Bebe's death. Then you can brainstorm on how she might be able to help you."

"I appreciate it," I say.

"Oh, and there's one other thing I need from you and the justice department." It's said as such an afterthought I don't give it much thought until he actually tells me what he wants. "In exchange for Bebe's help on this, I want her to get a full pardon for her crimes. I want it wiped off her record and her prison sentence expunged."

"I don't have that type of power," I say carefully.

"But you have access to the people who do," Kynan

points out as he skirts around the large table. "Make it happen."

I follow Kynan to the conference room door. "Anatoly is going to expect me back in New York as soon as he thinks Bebe's dead."

"Well, I can tell you I'm not letting Bebe go to New York to work on this with you. She either helps from the safety of Jameson or you don't get her help at all. You're going to have to buy yourself some time."

I ponder how to get more time away from Anatoly, and an idea comes to me immediately.

"Aaron," I say. Kynan stiffens, his expression darkening. I ignore it. "Anatoly suspects there's a kid, but I haven't confirmed it. I can tell him that I definitely think there's a kid, along with Bebe's mom, and suggest he let me go after them. It won't take much to convince him to clean up all loose ends."

"He'll think you're off chasing them, and you can be here working with Bebe to take him down," Kynan summarizes.

"Of course, you're going to need to send Aaron and Gloria away."

"Already thought of that," Kynan says. "I'm going to send them out to California to stay at my wife's house. I'll send a few of my guys to protect them, too."

"Sounds like a plan," I say, sticking my hand out.

He studies it for a long moment—to the point I

think he's going to ignore it—but then we're shaking on it.

I've just become partners with Jameson. Outside of my issues with Bebe, I can't help but think this was a really good change of events for me.

CHAPTER 10

Bebe

S TARING INTO THE bathroom mirror, I wonder how my life got so fucked up so quickly. I had genuinely thought all the bad stuff was behind me. I had thought I'd paid for my crimes. My life was finally getting back to normal. Less than twelve hours ago, I actually thought I might have a chance at a relationship.

That's gone now. I've been hiding in the bathroom for a good fifteen minutes, not wanting to have to walk out of here and confront that.

We'd stepped out of the conference room at Kynan's request. Dozer, Cruce, and Saint stared worriedly at me, but I gave the men my back, hurrying off to the women's bathroom. It's true Griffin Stoltz or Moore—whatever the fuck his name is—has thrown me for a loop, but truth be told, I'm far more shaken up to know that Anatoly Bogachev is after me.

Bile had actually risen in my throat, coating it with a burning sour taste when Griff told me that he was hired by Anatoly to kill me. It instilled fear deep within me, as it should. He's an incredibly dangerous and cruel man.

Memories of the last time I'd seen Anatoly—a surprise visit he'd made to Boston to bestow upon his most prized hacker the importance of obedience and loyalty to his organization. My stomach turns with nausea from those memories and I lean over the sink to splash cool water on my face. It helps to wash away the unbidden tears.

Turning the water off, I grab a handful of paper towels from the dispenser and pat my face dry. My red-rimmed eyes stare back, giving me no answers on what I should do at this point.

The bathroom door opens, and I find myself not giving two fucks who might be walking in and catching me having a personal moment. Not surprised when I see Kynan poking his head in.

"Hey," he says gently, his gaze taking me all in and perhaps lingering a little longer on my tearstained eyes. "Imagine all that was quite a shock to you."

"That may be the understatement of the year," I say with a humorless laugh. I turn back to the mirror, leaning forward to rub my fingertips under my eyes. Taking a moment to peruse my appearance, I'm satisfied I don't look too horrible and twist the water back on to wash my hands.

Kynan comes into the restroom, letting the door swing shut behind him. Resting a hip against the sink, he crosses his arms over his chest. "So, what's the play? Want me to kill the FBI guy? At the least beat the shit out of him for you?"

My brows furrow, and I give him a sharp look. "Of course not. He was just doing his job."

"Oh come off it, Bebe," he chides. "You're pissed."

"No, I'm not," I insist, but I'm unable to hold his gaze. I focus on scrubbing my hands as I admit, "Okay, yeah… I'm pissed, but for different reasons than him being an undercover FBI agent."

Kynan jerks his chin with surprise. "Like what?"

"Like…" I immediately falter, feeling awkward talking about this with my boss. But Kynan is a bit more than that. He set me free from prison. I trust him more than probably anyone else in my life. I take a long, deep breath before turning to him. "He got close to me in a short period of time. Insinuated himself into my life—"

"To protect you," he points out.

I roll my eyes. "Yes, I get that. But he didn't have to do it that way. He could have figured out what he needed to know just by watching. He didn't have to get personal with me and Aaron. I don't like people playing games with me."

"Unless he wasn't," he suggests thoughtfully. "Maybe this was more personal to him too."

I shake my head bitterly, turn the water off, and reach past him for some hand towels. "Whatever. All I want to do is go after Bogachev. Fuck the FBI... I'll bring him down."

Kynan just stares at me, evaluating my request. "I get your anger. You're bitter toward Bogachev. He made you steal nuclear codes, then put you in a horrible situation where you had no choice but to get caught and take the fall to protect your country and your son. And now he wants you dead. You have every right to hate him and want to take him down."

"Glad you see it my way," I reply tightly as I toss the used towels in the garbage and start toward the door.

Kynan stops me with his hand on my elbow. "You know, you never really told me anything about your relationship with Bogachev."

"You never asked." My eyes stay locked on his, unwavering and steady.

"Griff was telling me a little bit about what he's learned while he's been undercover. Bogachev's network is vast. He has hackers working remotely for him all over the world."

"What's your point?"

"Just that Bogachev doesn't do face to face with his minions. He tells them what to do, ensures they get paid, and pockets the profit. I assumed the same with you, but I'm thinking you've met the man, haven't you?"

It's torture not to let my gaze drop, but I refuse to be cowed. His question is incredibly personal, yet I realize...

I already opened the door to the information Kynan is trying to solicit.

Gently pulling my arm away from him, I settle against the sink and punch my hands into the front pockets of my jeans. "Remember back in March when we were all out in California, trying to catch Joslyn's stalker?"

Kynan nods. It was about six months ago and I'm sure he hasn't forgotten a thing. He'd just gotten me released from prison. I, in turn, used my skills to pull off all kinds of amazing technological things to help Kynan catch the bastard.

"Joslyn was having a tough time dealing," Kynan says softly. Suddenly, I realize he knows what I'm getting ready to tell him.

I nod, continuing the story. "We were talking about when her stalker had broken into her house and was trying to kill her…"

"And you shared something very personal with us," Kynan murmurs.

Yes, I had. I'd shared it so Joslyn could have hope that everything does eventually get better with time. I had admitted to both I'd been raped before, and I understood the terror of reliving those moments.

"My attacker's eyes were bloodshot," I'd told Joslyn. "I don't know if maybe he was lacking in sleep or maybe he was on drugs, but for the longest time, I would have nightmares about those bloodshot eyes. Except in my dreams,

they weren't naturally red. More like supernaturally red. My point in telling you is I promise—over a period of time—those memories will lessen significantly as you process and deal. I can't say you'll ever let it go, but it will get easier."

"So you know," I whisper, my tone almost pleading. "About why I want to take this fucker down."

"Because he's the one who raped you."

I nod, finally giving up the fight to hold his stare. "I wanted out, Kynan. Told Anatoly I was out. He came all the way from New York to Boston to impress upon me that one doesn't simply walk away from Anatoly Bogachev. He wanted those nuclear codes, and well… he wanted other things as well."

"I'm so fucking sorry, Bebe," he says as his hands clench into tight fists. I can tell by his expression he wants to wrap me up in a hug. He doesn't, though, because he knows me well enough to realize I couldn't handle it right now. I'm tough. I'm a survivor. I take pride in having survived the hell Bogachev put me through, and I'll crumble if he shows me the slightest bit of empathy.

Instead, I lift my chin and give him a brave smile. My words are true and confident, and I mean them with every breath inside of me. "He hurt me. Terrified me. Threatened Aaron. I was willing to give him a pass. Hold my tongue and keep my end of the bargain—meaning I'd keep quiet and take the fall if my family stayed safe. But he's coming after me now. He took a part of me I can't get back, then robbed me of years of my life with Aaron. That fucker thinks he can do that and I'm going to take it willingly? Well, I'm not. I'm taking him down whether you give me the okay or not."

"You have the okay," he assures me, and I blink in surprise. That was easier than I thought. "However, you have to work in conjunction with Griff. He's got a long-standing investigation and a lot of information for us. It has to be done legally, Bebe, so we make sure Bogachev goes to prison forever."

I grimace because while I'm doing a good job confronting my feelings about Bogachev, I'd prefer to never think about Griff again. "I don't need his help."

"But you'll take it anyway." His expression tells me he's not kidding about this. "You work with the FBI, Bebe, and you stay as aboveboard on this as you can. They're building a strong legal case against Bogachev, and you can't jeopardize that. More importantly, in exchange for your considerable talents, I've asked the government to pardon you in exchange for your help, so it's even more essential you play by the rules."

"What?" I rasp, my breath suddenly clogged up tight.

"I've asked them to have you pardoned. Have your prison time expunged. I've asked for the fresh start you deserve, especially if you help them take down the mastermind to the nuclear-code scheme."

I close my eyes, stunned by the possibility, only to

snap my attention right back to him. "Will they really do that?"

Kynan shrugs. "I've asked. We'll see. But tomorrow, we start working with Griff and the FBI to figure out how to take Bogachev down as quickly as possible. Can you work with him?"

Can I?

That's the real question when my feelings about him are so damned muddled. I just don't understand why he didn't tell me the truth from the start.

And why... why did he let things go so far in his kitchen last night? I'm mortified I let him do that to me—that I opened myself up to him. That I wasn't smart enough to see through the ruse.

I'm so horribly embarrassed I let myself be fooled, and I'm not even sure I can look Griff in the face.

Of course, I can't tell Kynan any of this. I'm not about to admit to such shortcomings.

Instead, I give him my answer with what I hope comes off as complete confidence. "I can work with him. No problem."

"That's good," he says with a smile. "Because I really don't think the guy is disingenuous."

I hold Kynan's gaze a moment before finally saying, "Doesn't really matter. I can work on a professional basis with him, especially if it means getting my life back."

"Good," he replies, then makes a gallant sweep of his

arm toward the door. "Now, how about you get back to work? I've told Griff to meet us here tomorrow morning. We'll get started then."

CHAPTER 11

Bebe

M Y MOM BRINGS me a cup of chamomile tea as I sit curled up on the couch, staring at the unlit fireplace.

"Thanks," I murmur as she moves to the recliner in the far corner of the living room.

"How's Aaron doing?" she asks in a low voice so our words don't carry upstairs to him.

I shrug because I have no clue. A few hours ago, I came home from work and had to inform both my mom and my son they'd have to go into hiding because my sins had caught up to me once again.

I could have easily thrown Griff under the bus, making him out to be the bad guy, but when it boils down to it, I didn't want Aaron to blame anyone for this situation other than me. No matter that Griff stalked me, insinuated himself into my life on false pretenses, and then repetitively lied, the truth of the matter is the only reason he did it is because I'd fucked up long ago by choosing to commit my crimes.

Doesn't mean I'm not still pissed at Griff.

Oh, I'm so very pissed.

I can't stand being lied to, and he took it way too far by pretending to actually be interested in me on such a personal level. When I think about what we did in his kitchen last night, I'm absolutely horrified and ashamed because I fell for his line of bullshit so easily.

My mom took the news as I'd expected her to—with quiet grace and understanding. I wasn't sure how Aaron would feel. He was far too young when I was sent to prison to understand. As he grew up, his earliest memories were of going to visit his mommy in prison. What we've had over these last six months... this is all new to him. A normal life is something we've had to take day by day, and it's taken him time to get used to it.

And now... it's all been shattered again.

"Aaron says he understands." I take a sip of my tea, watching my mom over the rim of the cup. "But he's ten years old. What can he really understand about this?"

"He's a mature ten," my mom replies.

"He's going to hate me," I grumble.

"Nonsense," my mom growls. "He adores you. That child fully understands the mistakes you made and the reasons why you went to prison. He knows you've done nothing but protect him with your very life, and until this thing with that Russian man can get settled, he understands we have to go away to stay protected."

My eyes water a bit, and the misery in my heart is so heavy right now I almost can't breathe. My mom tilts her head, giving me a sympathetic smile. "I love you, Bebe. You're the best daughter I could ever hope for, and you're an amazing mom to Aaron. You keep your head up, okay?"

"Okay, Mom," I murmur with a forced smile. "I'll try."

There's a knock on the door and my head swings that way, wondering who it could be. I'm not alarmed it could be anyone nefarious as Kynan stationed two Jameson guys outside. Tomorrow, they'll be escorting my mom and Aaron out to California where they'll stay until Bogachev can be arrested. I'll be moving into one of the vacant apartments at Jameson headquarters.

My mom pushes up from her chair before I can react, striding to the front door. After she looks through the top pane of glass, she immediately pulls the door open. From my angle, I can't see who it is, but my body goes taut when I hear *his* voice.

"Hello, Gloria," Griff says in a humble tone. "Is Bebe around so I can talk to her?"

My mom, traitor she is, gives Griff a welcoming smile. She wasn't as bent out of shape about his perfidy as I've been when I told her the full story. She even understood him keeping his secrets until he couldn't possibly because he was undercover. Of course, she has no idea just how close he and I had gotten last night, which is really where the source of all my anger stems from. He let us cross a line, and he shouldn't have.

"Sure," my mom answers graciously, motioning for Griff to come in. He's got on his trademark biker, work-for-a Russian-mobster/cybercriminal outfit of faded jeans, long-sleeved dark Henley, and biker boots. His hair is loose around his shoulders.

I rise from the couch, balancing my cup of tea to face him. I don't even have the energy to glare anymore. Kynan spent a great deal of time today at headquarters, talking me off the ledge. I wanted nothing to do with Griff after his big reveal, but it turns out I'm going to be working in close proximity with him to help the FBI take Bogachev down. Kynan did leave the choice up to me on whether I would accept the assignment. I wanted to tell him to go to hell, but ultimately, I swallowed my pride and told him I'd do it. I wanted Bogachev behind bars because it meant I could return to a normal life and my mom and Aaron could come out of hiding. As it stands, I'm completely stoked to get started on bringing Bogachev down and getting Griff out of my life as quickly as possible.

"What are you doing here?" I ask. We're set to meet tomorrow at Jameson according to Kynan, so I'm bewildered why he'd even bother to step foot here.

"I wanted to talk to you in private," he replies softly.

"Make some apologies."

"No need," I quickly say. "Let's just forget everything that happened and move on."

"Yeah," he mutters, running his hand through his hair and shooting an apologetic glance at my mom before pinning me with a hard look. "I can't forget what happened last night. We need to talk about it."

My mom whips her head toward me, her gaze questioning. My face flushes at the implication he's just left my mom with.

With a startled shake of her head, my mom starts backing toward the staircase. "I think I'll just go up to my room for a bit. Give you two some privacy."

I sigh. No sense in telling her not to go. She's silently projecting by her actions she wants me to get this resolved, so I nod toward the kitchen. "Want some tea or coffee?"

"No thanks," Griff replies with a polite smile.

"Then sit," I say, motioning toward one of the two guest chairs or my mom's recliner. I settle back down into the couch, then take another sip of my tea while Griff ignores the chairs and sits on the couch beside me, angling his body so we're face to face.

It's too close for comfort, yet I can't seem to move. But I do want this over with, so I get him on track. "You said something about apologies."

"I'm not sorry about hiding my true identity from

you," he begins, and I narrow my eyes. Not what I was expecting. "I was undercover. I didn't know if you could be trusted. I had years of extremely dangerous work under my belt I couldn't afford to blow."

"Anyone ever tell you that you suck at apologies?" I mutter.

He ignores me and continues. "I'm also not sorry I insinuated myself into your life under false pretenses. I really enjoyed the time I spent with you. I particularly enjoyed getting to know Aaron and hanging with him. Mostly, I had to try to get to know you as quickly as I could, because I was trying to size up just how much danger you were in. I was trying to determine if I could trust you with my truth. My goal from the start—from the minute Bogachev ordered the hit on you—was to protect you and your family, which superseded my undercover work. I would have gladly given up my cover if it was the only way to keep you and your family safe."

Okay… that's distinctly not an apology and yet, his words actually touch me.

"What I do regret," he says with a long sigh, "is in not revealing everything to you last night, after we…"

I hold up a hand, face burning again. "No need to say it. I know what we did."

"I wasn't playing a part, Bebe," he says, leaning toward me slightly. His eyes burn into mine, the green darkening with intensity. "Last night, in my kitchen…

with my fingers inside of you. That was just me and you. Had nothing to do with my case or your history. I wanted to give that to you. You wanted it from me. But the minute I took something personal for myself, I owed you the truth. I'm sorry I waited until this morning and caught you so off guard, but I really just needed some extra time to sleep on it. To determine if I was truly ready to blow my cover and go home in defeat."

"But you're not going home in defeat," I point out, suddenly feeling a bit sorry for him. "We're going to work with you to take Bogachev down."

"Yes," he agrees with a flat smile. "But I didn't know that last night. Or this morning when I showed up at Jameson. I thought my case against Bogachev was up in flames the minute I revealed myself. I had intended to come in, reveal my work, and then try to get you into some type of protective custody."

This explanation truly hits me deep in the middle of my gut. I had not considered what Griff stood to lose from this. I was too angry I'd started to fall for a man who was not who he said he was. I had assumed he had no feelings whatsoever for me.

"I want you to know," I say with careful consideration as to how to frame this. "What we did… the intimacy we shared… I don't just do that with anyone. I mean… I trusted you enough to open myself up."

"Sort of figured that out about you, Bebe," he replies

gently.

"And to find out everything I knew about you was a lie—"

"Not everything," he points out. "I told you so much truth about me. My background… my family life. The things we have in common and the things we don't. All that stuff we discussed… all real. I lied about my full name and what my purpose was in Cranberry. Everything else was the real me."

My gaze drops down to my cup, and a heavy realization settles in. "I lied to you, too. I lied about what I did for a living. About my history… being in prison. I was afraid to tell you because I was afraid you wouldn't like me if you knew the horrible things I'd done."

Griff's hand takes mine, and it forces me to look at him "I'm sort of fumbling, Bebe. I didn't expect someone like you to come into my life. Frankly, the timing is fucking awful, but I'm sure as hell glad Bogachev sent me. Anyone else, you'd be dead right now. Anyone else, and I wouldn't have met you. I'd just really like to know you forgive me for my duplicity. I need you to know that while a lot of what was going on between us was built on lies, there was a lot that wasn't. I hope you can see the difference and forgive me for maybe letting things go too far last night."

And it's suddenly clear to me. I'm not angry anymore since I now know what we shared intimately wasn't part of the ruse. That it was genuine.

"I can see it," I admit.

Griff just stares a long, hard moment, seeming to judge if I really mean that. Finally, he nods in acknowledgment and rises from the couch.

"Listen," he says hesitantly, glancing at my staircase. "Think I could talk to Aaron? I assume you've told him everything, and well… I want him to know exactly what I just told you. My friendship with him was as real as it gets. I need him to know that."

"Yeah, of course," I reply quickly, rising from the cushions. I can't pretend my heart isn't squeezing in awe over his thoughtfulness.

I lead Griff up the stairs to Aaron's room. After I knock on the door, I only open it after he calls out it's okay to do so.

Stepping inside, I find Aaron on the bed—on his stomach—reading a book.

"Aaron, honey," I say, and his gaze swings to me. "Griff is here. Wanted to talk to you."

Aaron's eyebrows rise. He sits up on the bed, looking past me to Griff with interest. There's no anger on my kid's face, but there's a whole lot of curiosity. He had a million questions today when I told him who Griff really was and why he was here, most of which I just couldn't answer.

Griff moves past me into the room, and I step into

the hallway to give them privacy, leaning against the wall. I shamelessly eavesdrop through the open doorway.

"Hey, buddy," Griff says, and I can imagine him holding out his hand to fist bump my kid. "What are you reading?"

"*The Last Olympian*," Aaron replies. I smile because I adore that my kid loves to read. I wasn't a big reader at his age, and it brings me joy that he's interested in it.

"Any good?"

"Yeah," Aaron replies. "It's the last book in this series and my favorite so far."

"That's cool," Griff says, and I can hear the hesitancy in his voice. "So… um… I wanted to apologize to you about all this mess going on."

"Why are you sorry?" Aaron asks, but not in a disgruntled way. He's genuinely curious, and that's probably because I didn't place any blame at Griff's doorstep when I explained what was going on. My anger stemmed from issues personal to Griff.

"I just hate you and your family have to be disrupted by this bad guy, but I want you to know I'm going to work hard to bring him down. Then you will be safe and can go back to your normal life."

"Yeah… my mom's pretty upset about it," Aaron says sadly, and my heart twists. "She's had it rough, and I just wish this was all over."

"Soon, buddy," Griff promises. "Your mom is one of

the smartest people I've ever met. With her help, we're going to have enough evidence to arrest this guy and put him away forever."

"And you'll watch over her and make sure she's safe?" Aaron asks. My kid… looking out for me when he's the child and I'm the adult. Tears prick at my eyes.

"Don't you worry. You and your grandma just have fun in California while we put this matter to rest."

"I've never been to California before," Aaron says.

"I have," Griff replies, and I hear Aaron's bed creak to indicate Griff has taken a seat. "There's all kinds of great things you can do out there."

I move down the hall toward the staircase to let them continue their talk. I'm assured Griff said the right things to my son and further satisfied that Aaron seems to be taking this upheaval in stride. I'm thinking maybe he deserves a trip to Disney or something when this is all said and done.

My future is decidedly undecided. My world has been turned upside down, not just by some megalomaniac who decided I'm better off dead now despite the fact I've held my tongue for the seven years I was in prison and haven't named him as a conspirator in my crimes, but by a tall, built, gorgeous biker dude who turned out to be an FBI agent.

I can't reconcile how I feel about Griff and the pure fear facing me as I struggle to get my life back in order again.

The only thing I know is the sooner we take down Bogachev, the sooner I can at least get back to what my normal used to be.

CHAPTER 12

Griffin

ONE OF THE guys that was in the conference room yesterday meets me at the steel gate of the Jameson building. Kynan had not bothered to introduce me to anyone. By the glares I'd gotten from all the men in the room, I took it they didn't really care to be introduced.

But this morning, Saint Bellinger seems amiable enough as he shakes my hand and introduces himself. Handing me a small fob with a digital passcode, he says, "That changes every four minutes, but it will get you through the gate here."

I follow him through the underground garage to a heavy steel door where I watch in fascination as he unlocks the door with a retinal scan. I'd seen Kynan do it yesterday, but I didn't feel comfortable remarking on it.

Not so right now.

I want to learn everything I can about this organization I'm going to be working with. "That's pretty high speed," I say off-handedly.

"You wouldn't believe some of the things Bebe and

Dozer have come up with for us," he replies. "I'm not sure if they'll add you to the retinal scan, but if not, someone will come let you in each morning when you arrive."

"Dozer?" I ask, wondering who the other half of what must be a dynamic duo is.

We enter the bottom floor, which looks like nothing more than an abandoned warehouse with graffiti on the walls and litter strewn about. It's a cover for what this building actually holds.

"You saw him yesterday," Saint replies over his shoulder as we move to the freight elevator that will take us up. "Black guy... super good-looking, annoyingly smart, and very protective of Bebe. Don't be surprised if he's an ass to you today."

"Duly noted," I reply, and I have to wonder... why is he super protective of Bebe? I don't like the surge of jealousy that rears its head over someone being close enough to be protective of her. I'd sort of assumed she was a loner given the things I've learned about her and her history.

We get off at the second floor, and Saint leads me to the same conference room we were in yesterday. He explains this floor holds the offices, conference rooms, and workstations. The third floor has a firing range and was previously where Bebe and Dozer developed their tech, but that's been moved to a sub-basement level.

"And the fourth floor?" I ask, having noted just how tall the building was in my prior visits.

"Private quarters, communal living area," he replies. "Bebe moved into one of the apartments this morning."

"And Aaron and Gloria?"

He throws a genuine smile my way because he can hear the concern in my voice. "On a flight for California with two of our best agents, Jackson Gale and Ladd McDermott. They'll be safe until we can handle this shit with Bogachev."

We wind our way through a maze of desks, some manned with people diligently working at their computers. The conference room comes into view, and I can see Bebe, Kynan, and Dozer in there. Bebe's huddled over a laptop, Kynan's scrolling through his phone, and Dozer is pacing. They all look up when Saint opens the door and motions me in. He doesn't stay, shutting it behind himself, presumably having more important things going on.

Kynan gives me a short smile, then nods toward the seat next to Bebe. First, I take the opportunity to introduce myself to the man sitting on her other side, who only stares impassively.

I move to him, holding my hand out. "Griffin Moore."

Dozer looks down to my hand, then back to me, his jaw locked and his eyes clearly refusing to accept civility.

To my surprise, Bebe elbows him hard in the ribs.

"Goddamn it, Bebe," Dozer grumbles, rubbing at his side.

"Be nice," she warns him, then looks up from her computer to give me a smile.

Dozer reluctantly takes my hand and shakes it. "Dozer Burney."

"Good to meet you," I reply, then move past him to the seat on the other side of Bebe.

"Dozer is our master strategist," Bebe advises me. "He's smarter than most people on the planet, and Kynan stole him from NASA."

Interesting. His brainpan alone makes him more compatible with someone like Bebe.

Moving to the head of the table, Kynan sits. "I sort of wanted to just brainstorm this morning. We need to figure out the best way to fake Bebe's death in a way that's convincing to Bogachev. We need to offer up proof so he buys it, then we need to figure out the best way to take him down."

"I've been giving that a lot of thought," Dozer says, leaning back casually in his chair, tapping his fingertips on the armrests. "We can build as much fake background on Bebe as we want, so why not give her an addiction like heroin? A few fake arrests for possession, then we set up a fake overdose. It fits with her story... years in prison, life destroyed. Why wouldn't she be an addict?

Griff can sell it to Bogachev as a low-risk murder so there won't be the same suspicion as if he'd put a bullet in her head or something."

We all look around the table at each other, searching for any issues with this idea. Kynan finally says, "I like it."

"I'll have our Pittsburgh field office coordinate with the local law enforcement in Cranberry. A fake news article on her death would be icing on the cake."

Bebe sort of slumps in her chair, muttering, "Yeah... it's just great. Aaron's friends and their families are going to learn I'm a heroin addict who died an ugly death."

"That will all be corrected once we get Bogachev in custody," Kynan points out.

But I can't stand the expression on Bebe's face right now. "We don't have to go that far with it. I can just take some pictures of you dead on a couch with a needle hanging out of your arm or something. Explain what I did to Bogachev. It should be enough."

Bebe gives me a wan smile. "Then we can get down to the real work."

"Except Bogachev is going to expect me back in New York as soon as I tell him Bebe's dead." I give my attention to Bebe. "How long do you think you're going to need to work your magic?"

"Well, a lot of that is going to depend on the security he already has in place. He's never going to fall for a phishing scam that would let us plant a virus through his email. Plus, I'm positive he has the absolute best anti-virus that's out there on the hacking market plus double firewalls, etcetera. So our best move is to try to access his system remotely through his Wi-Fi and that's going to take some modifications, depending on the type of router connection he has. This isn't going to happen overnight, but I think with some hard work, trial and error, and really good decryption coding, maybe a week… two at the most. All you need is imaging of the data, right? Not the actual data itself."

"Correct," I say, but give a frustrated shake of my head. "But we're going to have to figure out something, because I can't stay gone for that long. He'll want me back in New York ASAP."

"Bebe doesn't need your help doing this," Dozer says, his eyes glinting with dislike. I have to wonder what it is I've done to garner this attitude from him. I feel like things are cool between me and Bebe, so they should be cool with him, right?

Unless… he has feelings for her and considers me a threat.

"He has to be here," Kynan tells Dozer. "It's his case so he has to be involved in all aspects for the information we get to have legal standing."

Dozer mutters something under his breath and I hope to fuck he's not going to be actively involved in the work Bebe and I will be doing together. There's only so much of his glares and snark I'm going to take before I throat punch the fucker.

"Griffin and I actually talked about this a bit yesterday," Kynan continues, looking directly at Bebe. "We need to buy him a few weeks' time so Bogachev doesn't expect him back in New York."

"And how do you plan to do that?" she asks.

"Aaron," I reply, which causes Bebe's head to snap my way.

"Aaron?" she asks, her face awash with concern.

"Bogachev had asked me if I'd seen your kid and of course, I lied and said I hadn't. But when I tell him you're dead, I can say there's evidence through your house your mom has Aaron somewhere, raising him away from you, but that y'all are still in close contact with each other. Just the hint to Bogachev you might have told someone else—namely Aaron and Gloria—about him will have him paranoid enough to send me to find them, too."

Kynan stares in consideration, then turns his attention to Bebe. "What do you think?"

"Yeah," she replies softly. "Bogachev is paranoid. It was always so difficult having a conversation with him. He'd watch you like a hawk. The slightest facial tick or change of expression, and he'd be doubting everything you'd just said. It won't take much to get him to fall for that."

Now… this surprises me. Normally hacking syndicates like this are nothing more than an extreme and far-reaching web of people who sit in the dark behind their computers and do the dirty work for the kingpin. Most never even know the real identity of who they work for.

"You've met Bogachev before?" I ask.

She nods stiffly, her gaze returning to her computer. "Yeah… a few times."

My eyes cut quickly to Dozer, who doesn't seem bothered by this information, then over to Kynan, who wears a slightly pained expression and I start to feel a sense of dread.

There's no time to explore why I'm feeling this way, because Bebe brings her eyes to mine and they're determined. "Bottom line… he's paranoid, slightly mental, and dangerous. I think if you can throw him off your trail for a bit, we'll hopefully be able to come up with something that will work, so this can all be over with sooner rather than later."

"And you're okay with me revealing Aaron to him?" I push. I won't do this if she has any hesitation. We'll just have to come up with something else.

Her expression is grim as she shakes her head. "No, I'm not exactly okay with that. But he could find that information out on his own if he wanted, and Aaron's safe in California with good protection. I think the risk is low, as long as we can take him down."

I nod in understanding, not exactly loving this idea, but knowing it's our best. "Then let's start brainstorming ideas."

"Why won't phishing work?" Dozer asks the room at large. "You have the capabilities to create something so realistic that it could fool him."

"Possibly," Bebe murmurs with a nod. "But unlikely. Plus, he'll have the most sophisticated anti-virus software program. And I'm not talking about the stuff you buy legally. Black hats have far more sophisticated anti-virus and malware programs to protect against the very viruses and such they create."

This would be true. "The software out there on the black market, created by hackers for hackers, is insanely good. Bogachev will have the best, which will ferret out anything that doesn't come directly from a legit source."

Dozer isn't put off. "Then go to a legit source and send it from there. I'm sure the FBI has the power to command such stuff, right? Find out where he banks, go there, and have them send him a communication with a virus—"

I cut him off with a shake of my head. "Can't involve privately held companies in a sting operation unless you have very convincing evidence that's not circumstantial in nature. So far, everything we have on him is circumstantial."

"His Wi-Fi is where we'll need to concentrate," Bebe murmurs, then immediately starts typing on her laptop. "It's guaranteed Bogachev is going to have sophisticated cybersecurity, so maybe rather than hacking him directly, we hack the company that provides his router updates, then install a virus in a security patch."

Dozer shakes his head. "But then *you're* opening yourself up to criminal actions. That's a hard no, Bebe. You should concentrate on perhaps building some type of jammer that will cause his network to go down temporarily, then maneuver something in that way."

Kynan leans forward, putting his palms on the table. "I think it's clear we've got our work cut out for us. Settle in, and I'll have some coffee and food sent in. I've got some other things I need to take care of."

He focuses on me. "When do you want to carry out Bebe's fake death?"

"This weekend," I say, glancing over to Bebe. She stares with those big blue eyes, completely unafraid of what she's landed herself in the middle of. I suspect she's been through so much that there's not a lot left to fear except for the well-being of her child, and Aaron is safe for the time being. I look back to Kynan. "Bogachev was getting insistent I move on it, and I've got to keep him satisfied."

Kynan nods. "I'm going to put a call into the Cranberry chief of police to see if we can set up a meeting. We should go there this afternoon to get them on board with this."

"Sounds good," I reply, feeling hopeful we can pull this off.

Kynan leaves the room, and Dozer leans forward past Bebe to address me. "So what's the deal with your image, dude? The long hair, beard, tattoos?"

"Called a cover, dude," I return dryly.

"Hmm…" he replies with a slight wrinkle of his nose, clearly conveying his distaste. The guy is clean-cut and impeccably dressed.

To my surprise, without looking up from her screen, Bebe says, "That worked out well for Griff's cover with me. I'm a sucker for the long hair and tatts."

I refuse to let my chest puff out, but I don't hide my smirk from Dozer. She clearly prefers her men to look a certain way, and I've got the upper hand there.

Of course, the hair and beard were part of my cover. Bebe would probably flip out if she saw me with a haircut and my standard government black suit.

Maybe one day… when this is all over, she'll have the opportunity to see that side of me. She'll be able to choose whether that pushes her buttons, too.

One day, maybe.

CHAPTER 13

Bebe

THE WAY I must die is disgraceful.

A heroin overdose on a Saturday night in a cheap apartment.

I've never taken an illegal drug in my life—never even smoked pot. Not much of a partier either. Those couple of beers I'd had with Griff the night before last is about as crazy as I get.

Yes, I'd rather go out in a blaze of glory like an execution—bullet to the back of the head—or having my throat slit in gory fashion.

Instead, I'm lying on the couch in Griff's apartment, my legs splayed, and a fake needle sticking out of my inner arm. Kynan hired a makeup artist who has effectively made my hair appear greasy, my eyes sunken, and scars on the insides of my elbows from repetitive use. We're staging the photos in Griff's apartment as the sparse decor goes more in line with a heroin addict versus the luxury of my house.

It's only Dozer and Griff here with me tonight. Dozer's snapping photos from various angles while Griff watches from the kitchen. He's been unusually quiet tonight, and I can't figure out if it's because this is just distasteful or he's biting his tongue because Dozer's been a dick to him all evening.

It's something that's been going on since the two officially met yesterday, and I'm getting sick of it. I know Dozer's offended on my behalf by Griff's duplicity, but he needs to let it go.

I have.

I just haven't had a chance to tell Dozer I've let it go. Haven't had a chance to tell him about Griff's visit to the house and his talk with Aaron, which truly… made all the difference to me.

I'm focused now on bringing Bogachev down, and I need Dozer to get on board. I need him to stop adding stress on top of it by having this beef with Griff.

"Just a few more," Dozer murmurs, moving in to take a close up from where I lay on Griff's couch. "Hold still, Bebe. Let's try a few with your eyes open if you can give me a good, unfocused death gaze."

I focus on the light fixture above me, then let my eyes go blurry. Dozer's iPhone makes a camera shutter clicking sound with every picture he takes.

"These are good," Dozer says as he starts flipping through the photos. "I think we've got enough that we can get out of this fucknut's apartment and—"

"Just what the hell is your problem, asshole?" Griff snarls as he advances on Dozer.

I jump up from the couch, the fake needle falling to the floor, and put myself right in Griff's path before he can reach my friend. When I put my hands on his chest, I feel the muscles leap under his shirt. He's got a very nice chest.

Griff doesn't even look at me though, instead glaring over my shoulder at Dozer.

"My problem," my best friend says from behind me, "is you led my girl on. Acted all interested in her, appealed to her girlie sensibilities so she'd invite you into her life—"

"Okay, now just wait a minute," I snap, turning from Griff to face Dozer. "I do not have girlie sensibilities."

Dozer ignores me, glowering at Griff.

I glance back at Griff to find him glaring at Dozer.

With a sigh, I give my regard back to Dozer, moving in close to him. "I need you to stop this. I'm not mad at Griff, so you shouldn't be."

"He used you—"

I cut Dozer off with a hand to his chest, opening my mouth to deny it. Before I can, Griff starts defending himself.

"What happened between Bebe and me is none of your fucking business, but if it gets you off my back, you need to know there was nothing fake in my feelings. What's between us is genuine."

I whirl to face Griff. He'd said that in *present* tense.

What's between us.

Not what *was* between us.

Is there still something there? He never gave me any indication there might be when he came to my house. We only spoke of the future in terms of taking Bogachev down.

"Whatever," Dozer replies dismissively then brings his eyes to me. "Come on. We got what we need. I'll take you back to your apartment at Jameson, then we'll choose the photo for him to send to Bogachev."

"I'll take her back," Griff growls.

"Jesus," I say, taking a step away from Dozer to put myself squarely in the middle of them again. "I want this shit to stop. It's stressful enough with what we've got to do. I don't need you two going at it."

Griff just stares stonily at Dozer, and he glares back.

Christ... they're children.

"Dozer," I snap, forcing his attention to me. "Let it go. I have. Things are cool between Griff and me."

I hold my breath to see what he'll do, and I'm discouraged when he mutters. "Yeah... whatever. I'm out of here. I'll text you the photos when I get home."

He storms out of the apartment and I only hesitate a moment before I run out after him. Catching him halfway down the stairwell, I reach out to grab his arm in frustration. "Dozer... why are you acting this way?"

He pivots to face me, a broad grin on his face. His hands come to my shoulders, and he pulls me in to place a hard, fast kiss on my forehead. "I'm all good, baby girl. But if you haven't noticed, my little display smacked of jealousy, which implies you and I might have a thing together. And *that* means the man in there will stay on his toes and not loiter when it comes to you. I don't want him getting complacent."

My jaw drops, and I mutter, "I don't understand."

"Girl, you are just blind." Dozer laughs. "That guy in there likes you, and I mean *a lot*. But he's also got this whole, 'I'm FBI and bound by duty, and I don't have time for romance' vibe going on. So I want to keep him on his toes. I don't want him to take you for granted, and the best way to do that is to make him think I'm interested in you and that's why I can't stand him."

I just blink at Dozer.

Repetitively.

"Now, if something happens between you two tonight after he takes you home, then you can thank me for it at work on Monday, okay?"

"I don't even know what to say to you right now."

"*Thank you, Dozer*, will suffice." He chuckles, then kisses me on my cheek. As he bounds down the staircase, I just shake my head.

I refuse to thank him for his matchmaking shenanigans, returning to the apartment still feeling bemused. Griff is standing in the middle of the living room where I'd left him. "No offense, but your coworker is an asshole."

I snicker. "He can be. But he's also my best friend."

"Not apologizing for the asshole comment," he mutters.

This makes me laugh. "Wouldn't ask you to. And might as well just confess it to you, but Dozer was just acting that way to make you jealous."

Griff frowns. "What? Why?"

"Because he thinks there's something between us, but he doesn't want us to get lost in working on the case and ignore it. He thinks you're FBI, which to him means stuffy, and so you won't take advantage of the situation."

Griff looks ever so serious as he says, "Dude pointed out I've got long hair, a beard, and tattoos. I came here to stalk and kill you. How in the world can he even consider me stuffy?"

I snicker, giving him an appreciative once-over. He's as far from stuffy as can be, but still, I have to admit, "You're a Fibbie, and you guys *are* pretty strait-laced."

Griff gets a gleam in his eyes, taking a calculated step toward me. "So, if I were a stuffy, strait-laced FBI agent, I most certainly wouldn't do this, would I?"

My entire body braces to see what he'll do, and my

skin tingles from head to foot. No man has ever made me feel lightheaded before, but I go dizzy when his big hand comes to the back of my neck. Like weak in the knees, jello-legged, ready-to-collapse-to-the-ground kind of woozy. He moves in closer, dips his head, and brushes his mouth against mine.

In this moment, I realize I'd give him anything he asked from me. If I had more time to think on this, I'd think this might have to do with the fact I'm not only insanely attracted to him and beyond repressed sexually due to prison circumstances, but also because I trust him.

After all, he did save my life.

My entire body surrenders, sags right against him, and his arm comes naturally around my waist to hold me tight. The kiss is gentle, exploratory, and yet possessive at the same time. Griff is affirming he still has genuine feelings, and he's not afraid to act on them.

But then the kiss stops, and I don't know what any of this means. Without the pressure of his hand on my neck or his lips whispering against mine, I feel insecure and out of my depth. This man—almost a near-stranger—sent here to kill me, only to protect me instead, and now he's giving me an opportunity to put my past to rest once and for all. He kissed me, yet we should have a purely professional relationship, but I don't want to abide by rules that would have us maintaining a distance.

We're once again at a distance now that he's stopped kissing me, and I don't know if I even have a right to ask him to bridge it.

I'm not sure if it's my face, or perhaps he feels it in the slight stiffening of my body, but Griff frowns. "What's wrong?"

"I'm just…" Just what? What am I? "Confused as to what's going on between us."

"I thought me kissing you was pretty clear," he replies gently, his eyes probing mine for some type of acknowledgment I understand.

I'm more confused than ever.

When I pull away from him, Griff's hand releases my neck and falls to his side. "We've known each other a week and a half. We met in an unconventional way in a mishmash of lies and half-truths. Now we have to work together on an important case to bring down a man who ruined my life once and wants to do it again. I'm kind of thinking I've got the right to be confused by this. I mean… you and I have a job to do. It's important work. Should we even be kissing, or… other things?"

His grin is wide and teasing. "I don't know… depends on what 'other things' you have in mind."

Glaring, I stomp my foot. "I'm being serious, Griff. I need some clarity. I'm not the best person at communicating. I was very isolated for the last seven years. I'm withdrawn and introverted. Why I'm so good at coding and computers is because I understand them a lot better than people. When I got out of prison and reunited with Aaron, I didn't even know how to talk to him, but what I learned was I actually had to talk. I had to put things out there so they could be addressed. So I'm putting it out there to you… I need to know what this is. Something we should ignore until we bring Bogachev down? Something we should pursue? I need some guidance so I quit worrying about it."

Throughout my rant, I notice the grin slip off his face and his eyes darken a bit. Perhaps I stepped over a line. Maybe that came off as way too whiny and unattractive to such a self-assured man. Or it could be I'm just the world's biggest moron.

Griff's head bows slightly, causing his long hair to fall forward. He scrapes it back with his fingers, tucking it behind his ears. When his gaze comes back to me, I feel a settling deep down in my gut just from the expression on his face.

Lips curled slightly—not in amusement at my insecurity, but in understanding. Eyes warm, empathetic. Jaw set in a determined manner. I just know—deep in my gut—that the words getting ready to come out of his mouth are going to set the course of my relationship with this man.

"You want to know what this is, Bebe?" he asks, but I hold still because of the low, rhetorical rumble of his voice. "It's everything. It's fate. It's serendipity. It's fucking destiny. Our paths crossed, two people who were probably a billion-to-one odds of ever meeting, yet we were supposed to come into each other's lives at the moment we did. I was supposed to be the one who was sent to find you, and it was supposed to be you that I was meant to save, and together? Well, together the world is our fucking oyster is what I'm thinking. We're going to work together—take down the monster who destroyed your life and hurt so many other innocent people. We're going to do it together. And while we're at it, we're going to continue to get to know each other. And if I may be so bold as to say, I already have a fairly intimate knowledge of you and I intend to continue to get to know you. I don't need for this case to be over to take it to the next level with you, but if you want to take it slow, just know I'm not fucking going anywhere so we can move at a pace that's good with you. Whatever we decide—we do it together, knowing we're together for a reason that defies all logic and reason, and I'm not letting this opportunity pass."

I just stare at him, thinking my ovaries just might have combusted.

"Is that clear enough to you?" he asks.

Nodding, I continue to stare like a wide-eyed owl, wondering if I can get him to repeat that entire speech one more time so I can remember the exact details to tell

Dozer about it.

Griffin smiles again. This time, I can tell he's amused and thinks I'm the cutest thing ever. His hands go to my face, hold me in place, and he bends to kiss me once again.

It's deep, but not overly erotic. Promising.

All too brief.

He pulls away and when my eyes flutter open, he's regarding me somberly. "I'm going to New York."

Startled, my body jerks over such a proclamation. "But why?"

Griff's thumb grazes my cheek. "I want to make sure Bogachev buys my story of your death. I want to look him in the eye when I tell him how you died and that Aaron's still out there, and I should find him. I want to make sure he doesn't doubt me, and that it's safe to come back here and be around you, because I am not going to put you in danger. I really need to see it for myself."

Now I'm scared and it's not for me, but for Griff. I know how demented Bogachev is, particularly if he thinks someone is disloyal. "No, don't go. Notify him by phone. We'll both be safe at Jameson until I can figure out how to hack him."

Griff shakes his head. "Sorry, Bebe, but I need to do this. I need to judge the situation. While I need to do everything to maintain my case, I need to balance that with making sure you're absolutely safe."

And it's then I learn my first lesson about Griff. I can tell by the tone of voice there's no arguing with him about this.

But then I realize… this actually may be a golden opportunity.

"Will you be going to his apartment?" I ask.

"Yeah… he conducts all his business from his home."

"Then I have an idea," I say, my mind now spinning madly with inspiration.

CHAPTER 14

Bebe

"**H**AND ME THE solder thingy," I tell Dozer, holding my hand out like a surgeon requesting a scalpel.

"Solder thingy?" he asks. I can hear the smirk in his voice, but the tool is placed in my hand. I touch the tip lightly against the metal alloy, which hisses, melts, and secures the wire clip to the circuit board. "You should really learn the terminology if you're going to be using it on advanced circuitry."

I blow a soft breath over the board, not that it's needed. The alloy has already cooled and solidified permanently. "You know I fly by the seat of my pants on many things."

"Yes, I do know this about you," he agrees with a low chuckle. "Speaking of pants… did you keep yours on this weekend?"

Jolting, I shoot him a nasty glare over my shoulder. Not that what he just asked me was incredibly personal, but it's that he's just now getting around to asking me. He's been working by my side all morning, and he hasn't asked a damn thing about me or Griff. Hasn't even shown a single curiosity over Griff not being here, and now he just blurts out about wanting to know if I got laid?

"That's rude," I say primly before returning to my work. We're building a new satellite phone prototype for our teams to use when they're out on missions.

"Whatever," he replies, taking the solder thingy from me and setting it down. He reaches over, spinning my stool so I turn away from the circuit board and face him. "Now, I've been dying to know what the hell is going on all day, but you haven't said a damn word. I'm also hungry and going to go get some lunch, but I can't go wondering what the hell happened between you two after I left his apartment, and frankly... now that I'm thinking about it... you're the one who's rude for not having told me already."

He finishes, sucks in a deep breath because that was quite the mouthful, then motions for me to proceed.

I should make him wait for it, since he waited so long to ask, but truly... I've been dying to tell Dozer all about it. I feel it's only right given the fact he did the whole asshole thing with Griff to make him jealous and all.

Dozer watches me expectantly. I let him stew for just a few moments longer, then lean forward and quickly explain how everything went down. "Okay, after you left, I just went ahead and admitted to Griff you were trying to make him jealous so his interest wouldn't languish while we worked on the case, then I point-blank asked him if there were feelings between us and what we should do about it. He gave me a really great speech about destiny, then he kissed me and it was really good. You know, one of those sweet, romantic kisses, but it had that underlying hint that it could blow up into something so much more."

I smile—all big and cheesy—proud of myself for having taken control of my own fate and putting things on track in a way where I could at least know what to expect. I bet he's proud of me too.

Instead, he frowns. "But did it, in fact, blow up into something so much more?"

I roll my eyes. "Is sex all you ever think about?"

"Yes," he replies in a matter-of-fact tone. "And so should you. You need to get busy with that. You have a lot of time to make up for."

I consider this, and he would not be wrong about that point. But I'm also so far out of practice I feel like I'm a virgin again or something. Plus... I've got this inherent awkwardness about me having spent the last seven years so isolated from men and normal people in general.

On Saturday night, Griff didn't seem to be in a rush. In fact, he didn't press for anything more than a smoking hot kiss when he dropped me off at Jameson. He was going to leave early the next morning for New York, and we would not be in contact again until he was assured Bogachev was truly oblivious to what we were doing.

I'm not overly happy about him going to New York or the fact we won't be in contact. I'm scared something's going to happen. I had a horrible dream last night that Bogachev had actually been following Griff from the start, knew I was alive and well, and that Griff was working undercover with the FBI. I shudder when I think about the dark places my dream went to last night and the things Bogachev did to Griff.

But there is some merit in Griff wanting to do this face to face with Bogachev. He'll be better able to judge the situation, which will give us some added reassurances as we continue to work to bring him down.

I scrubbed Griff's phone for him Saturday night before he left Jameson headquarters. Removed every trace of me on it other than the two photos he chose to take with him, showing my death by drug overdose. In the off-chance Bogachev took a paranoid turn—which he often does—we didn't want him to insist on seeing Griff's phone and there be evidence of our past texts or phone calls. I also scrubbed Griff's Google searches and maps he'd used when he was stalking me.

That was probably all unnecessary, but it makes me feel slightly better about Griff going back into enemy territory.

I gave Griff one more thing to take with him. I'd brought him down to R&D, then gave him a small device that looked like nothing but a small USB storage device. "If you can get this into any electronic device with a USB port in his home, I can possibly hijack his Wi-Fi. A TV is a good option since the slots are usually in the back and well hidden."

Griff pocketed the device I had been working on, a project I had hoped would actually boost Wi-Fi signal strength but which I felt I could possibly use to communicate with once it was plugged in. I'd have to bust ass the next few days to work on modifications to the coding to see if we can use it to break through his security, but it was one more possibility if I couldn't get in another remote way.

"Not going to give me the juicy details, are you?" Dozer asks glumly. I blink in confusion, lost in my worries over Griff and his meeting with Bogachev.

I shake my head. "I'm sorry. My mind went elsewhere. I'm just worried about Griff going to New York."

"I take that to mean you did not get laid this weekend then," Dozer drawls, sliding off his stool. "I'm going to go out for lunch today. Feel like some Primanti's. Want to come? You can tell me what, if any, lame stuff you did with Griff?"

With a few taps of my finger, I log off my workstation and shake my head. "I'm going to grab a sandwich in my apartment while working on some coding for the jacker I gave Griff to try to plant in Bogachev's apartment."

We both head out, locking up R&D until we return. No one is allowed in here unless it's with Dozer or me—not even Kynan. As such, he doesn't even have a key to get in, although I suspect he could bust in with brute force if he wanted. Dozer heads to the garage while I take the elevator up to the second floor, swinging by Kynan's office to see if he's in. I want to run some ideas by him that I have for a new drone idea, but it's going to take a bigger budget than I currently have access to.

His office is dark and empty, so I move through the maze of agent desks toward the staircase leading up. I prefer to take the stairs when I can, mainly just to get a bit of exercise since I sit at a desk all day. The staircase itself is a work of art. The entire decor of our building is heavy with an industrial vibe. Sandblasted original red brick on the interior with exposed pipes and ductwork. The stairs are made of iron, cables, and reclaimed wood, and it seems to float upward through the second, third, and fourth floors. It even sways slightly if I bound up two steps at a time.

Just before I hit the first step though, I look across the space to a set of offices on the western side of the second floor. They're all made of glass, and I see Corinne

Ellery sitting at her desk in one.

When she catches my eye, she waves me toward her.

Corinne is actually the second Jameson employee I had met, although she wasn't technically a full-time employee back then... merely contracting with the company. Kynan brought her to the federal prison I was housed at in Fort Worth, Texas on that day roughly six months ago when he'd sprung me from my hell. I'd learned she was a psychiatrist whom he wanted there—apparently to gauge if my mind was sound.

At the time, it was a little offensive but in hindsight was probably a good idea. I was actually incarcerated at the Federal Medical Center Carswell, which housed mostly female inmates with medical and psychological issues. It was also home to the high-risk security female inmates. Given my hacking abilities, I was as high a risk as possible.

My seven years spent there, I was lumped in with a lot of other batshit-crazy women, some of which I'm sure probably rubbed off on me.

Regardless, Corinne and I get along really well and I consider her a friend of sorts. Since that time, she's come on to Jameson full time and works mainly in the area of criminal profiling, but she also provides mental health support to all employees. Some of the shit they go through is incredibly debilitating to the psyche. The most recent example is the fact we lost Jimmy and Sal to the botched mission in Syria, and Malik is still missing. Not knowing if he is even dead or alive is excruciating for most of us, and Corinne has been a busy lady talking through this with various employees.

I haven't seen her though.

It's a given fact I tend to internalize and process things on my own, which, granted, isn't the healthiest way to care for my mind.

I step into her office, but only enough to lean against the doorjamb. I assume she just wants to say a quick hello since it's been a while.

"Hey," she says, pushing her laptop aside. "Where are you off to?"

"Just up to my apartment to grab some lunch," I reply.

She nods. "Kynan told me what's been going on with Bogachev coming after you and all."

"Yeah," I reply with a somewhat frustrated sigh. "It sucks, but I hopefully won't have to stay here long."

"He said Aaron and Gloria are out in California."

"And of course I'm missing them terribly," I say with a humorless laugh.

"If you want to talk—"

She gets a chiding smile and shake of my head in return. "I'm good."

"I know this is a difficult time—"

Holding a hand up, I cut her off. She, however,

holds her own up.

"Just listen a moment, Bebe," she murmurs, her voice lilting in an almost-hypnotic way. "You've been through so much in your life. Ripped away from your family, isolated in prison, now with a mad man wanting to kill you while separated from your family again. It's a lot for anyone to handle. I just want you to know... it's okay if you're fearful, angry, resentful, or even ashamed by this getting stirred up again. It's natural. You should be drowning in an array of emotions right now. There's nothing wrong with talking them out with someone."

I don't like the fact that the first thing that comes to my mind after her little speech is a flashback memory of Bogachev raping me. Of all the trauma and misery I've endured over the years, that moment is one I believed had been firmly put to rest. Over the years, I had even managed to rationalize it was merely part of the punishment I'd deserved for getting involved with him and his criminal ways. He'd done it to show me his power and that he could hurt me without blinking an eye. He'd done it to keep me in line, and it worked. I allowed myself to get taken down, and I kept Bogachev's secrets because his lesson was imprinted deeply upon me.

But the rape itself, I had felt somewhat reconciled with. The memories of it had dulled. I dealt with the shame by convincing myself it was my atonement for the bad things I had done. I truly came to believe I'd deserved it. And then I shut it away and forgot about it.

For the most part.

Now Bogachev is back in my life, and it's clear it's rearing its ugly head. Sure… I'm incensed he's coming after me, demanding my life now so he stays safe. But now I'm starting to get pissed about what he did to me too. How low he brought me in that one vile exercise of power and brutality over me.

I'm pissed he made me think I'd deserved it.

Corinne's face is open and inviting. I know this shameful event would stay private between us if I wanted to tell her about it.

But I don't. Mainly because these feelings resurfacing are awful and sickening. I don't want to relive what happened to me. I don't want to talk about it. I'd like to sweep it back under the rug where I'd kept it, then let myself be healed by helping to take him down. Surely, seeing Bogachev behind bars forever would go a long way to soothing my soul, right?

"Listen," I say, pushing off the doorjamb. "I think I'm good right now, but if I feel the need to hash it out, I promise I'll come talk to you."

The way Corinne purses her lips tells me she doesn't really believe a word I say, but she can do nothing more than accept my word. She can't force me to talk as she's only a resource available to us.

"I'll catch you around, okay?" I say with a friendly

smile.

"Sure thing," she replies.

Spinning from her office, I head toward the stairs and bound up them two at a time, enjoying the slight sway. In my apartment, I eat a tuna fish sandwich and putter around on my computer, writing notes for potential new code strings to implement.

I also spend a great deal of time wondering what Griff is doing and if he's safe.

CHAPTER 15

Griffin

A NATOLY BOGACHEV LIVES in a fifteen-million-dollar Brooklyn apartment with gorgeous views of lower Manhattan. His family roots are in Brooklyn with strong mafia ties. But he sort of eclipsed those uncles and cousins who deal in extortion and money laundering. The money he makes from cybercrimes puts him in the penthouse—an eight-thousand-square-foot apartment—while his relatives lead a far less luxurious lifestyle.

I decided to play it blasé about the death of his nemesis, Bebe Grimshaw. I'd texted him late Sunday to tell him I was back in the city and had good news for him. He told me to be at his apartment at noon, and I was there fifteen minutes before, always habitually early because I know that impresses a man like Bogachev.

I wait for him where I always do, in his formal living room. His office is just down the hall, and I can see his door is firmly shut from where I sit on a vintage Victorian-styled sofa that's uncomfortable as hell and twice as ugly. But it's expensive, which is really all that matters to the man.

The door doesn't open. Anatoly leaves me to stew, and he doesn't beckon me into his presence until five after twelve because while he appreciates punctuality, he doesn't feel compelled to bestow it on others. It's just one way he loves to display his power.

"Stoltz," he bellows, and it carries through the heavy carved door of his office. I'd only ever given him my fake cover name of Stoltz. I have no clue if he ever did a background check on me or not when I first came to work for him, but I've got an extensive history built under that name by the FBI.

I push up from the sofa, the delicate wooden joints squeaking, and make my way down the parquet floored hallway to my boss.

Unsurprisingly, the door opens by another one of Bogachev's employees, a beefy Russian immigrant named Karl who speaks heavily accented English. Normally, I'm the guy who stands in this office to protect the kingpin from some crazed intruder should that ever happen, but with me gone, Bogachev is using this guy as my replacement. As soon as I enter, Karl exits and shuts the door.

Anatoly sits behind a hand-carved Italian desk with stunning filigree work on the sides. It's large enough it could be considered masculine, but it's so ornate in its details it just comes off as prissy. All that matters to my employer is it's insanely expensive, so it's worth it for him to sit behind.

His head bent over a stack of papers, he doesn't bother glancing up. I take a moment to survey the room—a roving gaze I've performed hundreds of times over the last few years. The office has dark paneled walls and custom built-ins, many of which hold a host of electronics and servers.

Anatoly works mostly off his laptop, which is closed on top of his desk. I'd kill to be able to log onto it for just five minutes. I dart my eyes over to the large flat-screen TV mounted to the wall and I know there's no way I can plant Bebe's device there while occupying the space with Bogachev.

I quietly take one of the chairs across from him, waiting for him to acknowledge me. It takes almost a full five minutes before he does. "You said you had good news."

"She's dead," I reply blandly. "Fortuitously found out she had a little drug habit. Watched her score some heroin in a bar one night. Decided to make it look like an overdose as I figured that would draw the least amount of heat from the cops. No one cares if an addict dies, right?"

Anatoly's eyes gleam with excitement, and I want to fucking pluck them out of his head. I pull my phone out, tap the screen, and hand it over to him. His gaze drops to the two photos I'd selected of Bebe, who looks deader than a doornail on my couch with that fake needle hanging out of her arm.

He stares hard at the picture, but not with doubt or horror. There is pure delight on his face.

God, I hate this fucker.

Finally, he meets my eyes and demands, "Tell me the details."

I expected this, so I recount a grisly story I'd come up with. It was overly dramatic and full of sadistic details, including how I watched her take her last breath, and Bogachev eats it up like a rich, creamy dessert.

"And you're sure there's no blowback on you?" he asks, cutting his gaze down to my phone one last time to take a long look.

"Totally clean," I assure him.

He hands my phone back, ordering, "Destroy those photos."

"Understood."

"You can return to regular duties tomorrow," he says with a magnanimous wave of his hand. "Take the rest of the day off."

"Appreciate it," I say dryly. "But there's another potential problem."

Bogachev's eyes narrow. "What's that?"

"I searched her house. She lived there alone but was clearly still in close contact with her mom and son. There were pictures of them all over, drawings from her kid on the fridge. I found some cards he'd sent with a California address, but it's a P.O. box."

He sits up straighter, eyes darkening as he listens.

"You've eliminated this woman," I explain in a neutral manner. "I don't know what your beef was with her, but you'd asked me about a kid before. I'm assuming he might be a worry to you. If you suspect she might have divulged anything to the kid or mother, you could have a problem."

The lines in Bogachev's forehead furrow deeply as he ponders this. He sits back in his chair, clasps his hands behind his head, and stares at the ceiling.

Finally, he levels his gaze on me. "Go take care of it for me."

And just like that, he's ordered me to go murder a kid and his grandmother. While I know the feds want details on the cybercrimes I'm investigating, I'm sure hoping there are some conspiracy-to-commit-murder charges lumped in when this is all said and done.

I rise from the chair, then turn toward the door.

"Stoltz," he calls. I glance back with my hand on the doorknob. "You take care of this, and you'll have a nice bonus coming your way next paycheck."

I give him a curt nod in silent gratitude. He expects nothing more.

After exiting his office, I wait until Karl walks back in and shuts the door. I scan the hall to the living room, considering my next move. There are no electronics in there that I could plug Bebe's USB device into. The kitchen has a TV, but his personal chef will be making use of the space to prepare his lunch as well as his evening meal. Anatoly is obsessive about food, and he keeps a pricey full-time chef on staff at all times. Of course, he's obsessive about his physique too, and because of all that good food, he keeps a personal trainer on full-time retainer as well.

Glancing back to his office, I consider the habits of the man I've come to know well over the last two years. He eats precisely at one. He'll do so in the kitchen, unless he has plans out of the apartment, which is not rare, but it's not common either. While he eats, he'll lock his office. Whoever is on duty with him today—which would be Karl—is expected to eat in the kitchen as well, and they are always provided a plate by the chef.

I glance at my watch. It's twenty minutes past twelve, which means I should theoretically have time to plant this device somewhere else in this apartment. There's no guarantee Anatoly will stay in his office. He could have another meeting scheduled or even decide to go out for lunch.

On top of that, he has internal cameras everywhere, but he does not have someone actively watch the feeds. They are there—like any typical security system—to identify intruders after the fact. There's no need to watch what goes on inside his apartment during the day because Anatoly would never expect one of his faithful lackeys to be disloyal in any way.

Fuck it.

It's now or never. I need to give Bebe the best chance possible to dig into his computers.

Pivoting sharply, I hurry the opposite way down the hall to the large master suite. The double doors are closed but never locked. I stride into the room with purpose, acting as if I own the place. The best way to promote efficiency in undercover work is to move with utter confidence. I close the door behind me, leaving it cracked just an inch so I can keep an ear on the situation outside the room.

I'm not overly familiar with Bogachev's bedroom, only having been in here maybe five times and usually only to grab something at his request. But I do know he has built-ins that house a large, flat-screen TV. I move quickly to the unit, dismayed over the minimal lack of clearance between the edge of the TV and the edges of the custom-built cabinetry. The TV is mounted to the wall and pulls out slightly, but not enough to give me a clear view.

I can't quite see the ports, so I have to quickly wedge my fingers around the edges of the television. I make it around one time without finding anything, realize I'm moving too fast. Taking a deep breath, I start another search, moving my way around the back portion of the TV, reaching as far back as I can without being hindered by the cabinet edges.

Finally, I stumble upon slight divots and know I've hit the right spot. It takes more careful examination to determine the difference between the HDMI slots and those for the USB cables. Two of the five slots are already housing cables, and I locate what I think is the correct port. I pull Bebe's device out of my front pocket, remove the cap that covers the plug-in portion, and maneuver it into the slot.

I breathe out a sigh of relief, push the TV back into place, then immediately break out into a cold sweat when I hear Anatoly's office door open.

His booming voice filters down the hall, coming through the crack of his bedroom door. "Those mother-fuckers think they can be late with my product and not suffer the consequences?"

No clue who he's talking to, but it's clearly someone on his cell phone. He doesn't talk business with his muscle.

My entire body freezes and I hold my breath, waiting to see if his voice gets closer to the bedroom door. There's no way I can legitimately explain being in here. And hell, all he has to do is glance this way to see the door is opened just a crack. If he does, he might come this way to check it out.

"You tell Kolisnyk he has until close of business today to come through or he's going to be sipping his cheeseburgers through a straw for a long time coming," Anatoly promises darkly. That means Karl will be having a visit with Kolisnyk later this evening if he doesn't comply, and Karl's knuckles will be busted up nicely from breaking the guy's jaw. I grimace in distaste, having had to carry out those orders for Bogachev before.

I hear nothing. My ears strain to pick up the sound of footsteps if they start coming this way, but it's just silence.

And then finally, from farther away—somewhere in the living room I think—Bogachev continues talking into the phone. My body relaxes when he says, "Yeah… eating an early lunch, then heading out for an appointment. Call me later."

An outflow of air gushes from my lungs. I move quietly to the door, thankful for the thick carpeting in his room, and put my ear up to the crack. I hear muffled voices now, so I assume everyone is in the kitchen.

Carefully, I open the bedroom door enough for me to slip through, and I slowly pull it closed behind me. I turn the knob as I do so, muffling the clicking sound of the latch. When I release it, I let out another breath of relief.

Walking calmly but assuredly down the hallway, I pass Bogachev's office. I don't spare it a glance, knowing the door will be locked. He never leaves it accessible to anyone but himself.

Hitting the living room, I cut my eyes across to the entryway to the kitchen. I can only see a portion of the island and fridge, but the clink of dishes and silverware says Bogachev is being served. Heading toward the door, I take two steps before a heavily accented voice stops me in my tracks.

"What are you still doing here?" Karl asks.

Glancing over my shoulder, I see him walking out of the kitchen. My expression remains bland as I jerk my thumb over my shoulder. "Had to use the john."

He frowns, but he can't really dispute it. The bathroom is in the same hallway as Bogachev's office. The Russian just nods, because I can tell he doesn't have the smarts to question me past that.

I don't acknowledge him further. Instead, I stride toward the door with an easy grace as if I have every right to be in Anatoly's home. If Karl were smarter, he would go check the camera feeds, so let's just hope he's not a proactive go-getter who has me fooled.

Regardless, I've got free rein to leave New York and return to Pittsburgh. I'm definitely anxious to get back to see what magic Bebe can whip up to help me take this fucker down.

But more than that, I'm just as excited to get back to Bebe.

CHAPTER 16

Bebe

"DON'T YOU EVEN work anymore?" I hear teasingly from behind me, and I tilt my head way back on the couch to see Anna exiting the elevator into the communal area on the fourth floor. Always nice to see her, but better yet… she has her three-month-old daughter, Avery, in her arms.

Tossing the magazine I'd been perusing on the coffee table, I roll quickly off the couch, bounding to my feet. "Give her to me," I demand, making grabby hands at the baby.

Laughing, Anna brings her to me and we make an effortless transition. As I settle back down onto the couch, I put my nose to Avery's soft head and inhale. "God, I miss the smell of a little baby."

Anna snickers, then plops on one of the chairs. Admittedly, I'd knocked off work a little early today, but it's never something I'd apologize for. I give Kynan a good sixty-seventy hours most weeks, and he'd never begrudge me time away from my desk when I'm frustrated.

And I am frustrated. I haven't heard from Griff in almost three full days, which has my anxiety flaring.

I tickle Avery under the chin, and she smiles before blowing a bubble out of her mouth. Leaning in closer, I baby talk to her. "Who's the cutest little girl in the world? You are, that's who."

Anna props her chin in the palm of her hand. "You're such a softy with her."

Which is a backward way of saying I'm not soft with others, which… that's legit. Shooting her a smirk, I bring my gaze back to Avery. "I just loved this age so much when I had Aaron. It went by way too fast."

"Speaking of which," Anna says as she leans forward a bit. "How are Aaron and your mom doing?"

"Settled in," I say, using the corner of my thumb to wipe drool off Avery's chin. "Anxious to come home, and I'm just as anxious to get them back."

Anna, of course, knows all about what's going on. As Kynan's right-hand man—woman—she knows everything around the office. In fact, she's become the go-to person for me to ask questions.

"What about Cage?" I ask. "Any word from him?"

"He checked in today," she replies glumly. "No leads on Malik at all, but Kynan's going to keep him there for a while. He's flying well under the radar though."

Meaning our government would not be happy to

find out Jameson has someone on the ground snooping around for our missing man. This trip is not sanctioned, but Kynan's never been one to play by the rules.

Glancing up from Avery to Anna, I take her in.

I mean, really look at her, and holy hell… she's gorgeous. She lost the baby weight but managed to keep some excellent curves. No clue if she had those before since none of us knew her before she got pregnant, but they're sexy as all get out. Her blonde hair is styled in soft waves, and she's actually wearing expertly applied makeup that makes her cheekbones stand out and her gray-blue eyes shine.

"Wait a minute," I ask while frowning, because none of this makes sense. "What are you doing here looking like a million bucks with your baby in tow?"

Anna chuckles. "I'm actually going out with some girlfriends tonight. They've been harassing me to get back out and have a life, you know? So I picked up Avery from daycare, then slapped some more makeup on. My mom is going to be swinging by soon to get her."

"Good for you," I cheer. Anna's been widowed for going on close to four months now. While I have no preconceived notions about when people should or shouldn't move on, I think Anna's ready. We've all watched her healing take place as she has worked here for Kynan. Part of that has to do with being a new mom with a baby she's deeply in love with. Avery is partly her father, and Anna has that amazing connection to him through her daughter. Over time, she laughs more, doesn't cry as much, and has genuinely insinuated herself into our work culture, becoming like a family member.

Moreover, she's become one of the biggest champions in keeping the torch alive for Malik. While Kynan is never going to stop searching for him, Anna is the one who keeps his memory alive for us. She barely knew him when he left to go on a mission with her husband, but since then, she's made it her job to be our very own eternal optimist about bringing him home. While she knows her husband isn't coming back, she's never given up faith we'll find Malik at some point.

"Why don't you come out with us?" Anna suggests with excitement. "It's just some friends I went to high school with, but we've all kept in really close contact. They're all nice and fun without being too annoying. Except Pauline. She's pretty annoying, but she's also rich and she'll buy drinks for us all night."

Chuckling, I shake my head. "No thanks. It's just not my thing."

"Going out and having fun isn't your thing?" she quips with a smirk.

I raise my head realizing... I'm not sure if it's my thing or not. I've not been "out with the girls" since long before I went to prison. I was a serious student at MIT, so all I did was study and hook up for casual sex to blow off steam. Then I got pregnant and had Aaron, so I didn't have time to go out. Then I began working for Bogachev... and my life started on its downward spiral.

"Oh my God," I say with a sudden realization. "I don't think I've been on a girls' night out since I was in high school."

Anna blinks in surprise. "Wow."

"No kidding," I reply slowly, actual awe over my lameness filling me.

"Now, you have to come," Anna urges. "It's not that it's not your thing, it's just you're way out of practice."

I consider her speculatively. Is it just that I need to get back into the swing of life again much in the same way Anna is trying to do since Jimmy died? Have I simply come out of prison to become a lazy human being who's just existing rather than enjoying everything life has to offer?

Maybe I should go out with her and her fun friends—except for the annoying Pauline who will spring for drinks.

I open my mouth, determined to do something different, but movement behind Anna catches my eye. Coming up the floating staircase is Griff.

As he trudges up the steps, his classic biker regalia of jeans, black t-shirt, and shit-kicker boots is revealed. His hair is pulled away from his face in a half-crown ponytail with the rest of his locks loose to his shoulders.

Anna spins to see what's behind her, and she murmurs, "Oh my."

I slowly stand from the couch, feeling a bit in a daze to see him so suddenly before me when I've been worrying so much for three days. Griff takes me in, his eyes roaming from my head to my toes, then settle on Avery. The corners of his lips curl upward, and his eyes go warm.

"Hello," Anna says brightly as she rises from her chair, taking a step toward Griff with her hand held out. "I'm Anna Tate, Kynan's personal assistant, and you must be Griffin Moore."

See… told you Anna knew everything that goes on around here.

Griff shakes her hand, giving her a charming smile. "Nice to meet you."

Then his fern-green eyes come my way, dropping to Avery for a moment before lifting again. "Cute baby."

"She's Anna's." I immediately grimace. Of course she's Anna's. Who else's baby would she be? But I find myself with a thick tongue and wanting to ogle him way too much, my relief he's safe is just that great.

There's a protracted silence as Griff stares. I can't stand his beauty, so I smile at Avery while Anna glances back and forth between us.

"Well," Anna drawls with exaggeration, taking the baby out of my arms. "I think my mom's here to pick up

Avery."

Total lie. Her mom was going to call when she pulled up, but I get what she's doing. She wants to give us some privacy.

"You sure you don't want to come out tonight, Be-be?" Anna asks, her gaze cutting to Griff with an amused twinkle to her eyes. "You'd have so much fun you wouldn't know what to do with yourself."

Griff swings his attention my way, but his expression remains bland.

Smiling at Anna, I shake my head. "I think I'm going to stay in for the night."

"Mmm-hmm," she responds. She's conveying so much in that tone that my cheeks heat.

Grinning, Griff ducks his head.

"I just meant Griff and I have work to go over," I hasten to assure her. "I need to get updated on his… um…"

My words falter. What do I need to get updated on?

"Mission?" Griff supplies, then flashes a mischievous grin.

"Yeah," I exclaim with my finger pointed upward. "Mission."

Anna shakes her head with amusement. "Okay, I'm out of here. See you tomorrow, Bebe, and nice meeting you, Griff."

He lifts his chin with a smile. "Yeah."

We both watch as Anna grabs her bag. With baby in tow, she steps onto the freight elevator.

When it rumbles out of sight, I turn back to Griff and give a long sigh of relief. "Thank God you're okay."

"I am," he confirms. "How have you been doing?"

There's warm concern in his tone, so I know exactly what he's asking. I give a tiny shrug. "I miss Aaron a lot. My mom, too, but I missed so much of Aaron's life that every day is just so precious."

"I can imagine."

Griff's eyes pin me in place.

"And I really missed you. I was so worried, but here you are."

"Here I am," he replies softly, his smile indicative of just how much he likes my words. "And I missed you, too."

CHAPTER 17

Bebe

S O, WE'RE ESSENTIALLY on a date tonight. At least that's what we've both decided to call it.

And truth be told, I'm sort of in hiding, so when it boils down to it, it's probably safer to stay inside the Jameson building. It would seem dating within the confines of our headquarters would make our options limited, but that isn't the case. We could have chosen to watch a movie in the media room, rack a game on the pool table, spend time on the beautiful rooftop area Joslyn decorated, or even head to the indoor gun range and get a couple of rounds in.

But given the fact the entire facility is riddled with strategically placed cameras for security purposes, I didn't want my date potentially televised to anyone. Not that there was anyone actively watching, but I could totally see Dozer pulling up the footage—perhaps (hopefully) seeing Griff kissing me—and making my life a living hell with teasing critique.

Which is why Griff and I are in my apartment,

watching a movie while lying side by side on my couch like a couple of teenagers.

It's odd, and I love it. The feeling of relaxation and security with him lying behind me, an arm casually draped across my hip, and his thumb lazily drawing circles on my jean-clad thigh.

We didn't start out here. First, I fed the man by ordering Chinese. We ate right out of the box using chopsticks, switching back and forth between lo mein and steamed dumplings. We ate and sipped at our beers, me sitting cross-legged on one end of the couch while he had the other, his legs stretched out, sock-clad feet on the coffee table.

We attended to business first, and he filled me in on his meeting with Bogachev. I don't think he left out any details because it was bad enough listening to him recount how he planted my USB drive into the man's bedroom TV and was almost caught doing it. I had terrible images flashing through my mind of Bogachev putting a bullet in Griff's brain for that little transgression, but it all turned out okay.

Not only did Griff successfully plant my device, but he also got Bogachev to send him on a fool's errand of a mission to murder my son and mother. It bought Griff the time he needs to come back here so we can put our heads together to bring this fucker down.

After that, the conversation moved more naturally

into other things that didn't have to do with murderous Russian mobsters and computer hacking. It was when Griff gave a mighty yawn I suggested that we perhaps watch a movie and if he happened to fall asleep on the couch of this little one-bedroom apartment, he would be well served by getting some rest.

With *Thor: Ragnarok* on Netflix and both of us avid Marvel fans, it didn't seem weird at all when he pulled me down into a supine position on the couch with my body in front of his. We're so perfectly fitted, and I cannot pretend to be unaffected by his big body molded to mine.

I settle into him a little more, wanting more contact. Moving his arm around my waist, he pulls me in for a hug of sorts while nuzzling his nose into my hair. Electric shocks tingle along my neck in response.

"You smell amazing," he murmurs, moving down to brush his lips across the sensitive spot right behind my ear. I can't help the audible intake of air, a mixture of being completely turned on and a little startled, only because I wasn't expecting it.

Griff continues to kiss his way down my neck with no hesitation whatsoever. His confidence is a complete turn on to me, knowing he wants this and he's taking it without asking. He moves his mouth to my shoulder, pulling the neck of my shirt to the side to expose the skin there. His right hand snakes its way under my shirt, his large palm settling on the center of my belly.

I'm assaulted by sensations from every direction—the touch of his lips, the warmth of his palm, the intense arousal between my legs. I know without a doubt I'm already soaked from just that little bit of affection. Ten and a half years is a long time to go without the regular touch of another human, and even though this isn't the first time he's touched me, it's still a new sensation to my body.

"Bebe," he whispers, lips making their way back up my neck to my ear. "Tell me what you want."

I groan, unable to articulate all the things I'm currently feeling. I want everything from him.

"Bebe," he repeats. "I want to make you come, but I need to know if you want that too."

"Yes," I hiss, unable to articulate much more, and he chuckles in response. I think I might have fallen a little in love with him, because his only thought is to bring me pleasure. I've never known a man like that.

His hand moves from my waist to expertly pop the button of my jeans. As he slowly lowers the zipper, my heart rate kicks into overdrive, causing my ears to buzz. This man drives me wild, and I'm not sure I'll ever get used to the feelings he invokes.

Sliding his hand into my panties, he works his fingers down, gently brushing past my clit and easily slipping inside. Some sort of mewling noise breaks free from my mouth as he pumps in and out, then slides his fingers up to circle my clit. He alternates between the two, changing up the rhythm and the pressure, dragging out the delicious feelings he's creating deep within.

As the sensations build and I edge closer to breaking, he continues to kiss any skin he can reach. My shoulder, neck, ear, chin, and my cheek. And as I fall apart under the expertise of his fingers, he whispers in my ear, telling me how beautiful it is to watch me come apart.

It's amazing the feelings another person can conjure within someone just by their words and gentle touch. Because what Griff just did to me was extremely gentle, and I loved it, but now I need more. So much more.

"Griff," I say with a little too much urgency if the way his head pops up is any indication. "I need you inside of me."

His nostrils flare as he sucks in a startled breath. "I'm only going to ask this once, then I'm going to take you at face value. Are you sure?"

I nod, reaching behind me to grab his impressive hard-on. And then it happens so quickly I'm not even sure how he managed it, but he's up from the couch, holding me in his arms and moving toward the bedroom.

Setting me gently on my feet next to the bed, he stares for a beat as if he's trying to determine his next steps. Then he breaks the stare, and a lecherous grin breaks across his face.

"Clothes. Off. Now," he says gruffly, and my body shivers at the raw desire in his tone. And while I'm not necessarily one to obey orders from someone who isn't my mom or my boss, this is one with which I'll gladly comply with.

I start disrobing while Griff does the same. After what feels like an eternity but was likely no more than a minute, we're both naked and I'm back in his arms, his lips on mine.

He devours me as he gently leans me back and down on the bed until I'm lying flat and he's bracing himself above me. Breaking the kiss, he makes eye contact.

"Bebe, I'm going to take this as slowly as possible, but if I get caught up in the moment and you need me to slow down, just say the word."

Then he's kissing my bare skin again, starting at my neck and working his way down. Across my collarbone and down to my breasts, where he spends a little extra time sucking and nipping and building a feeling of complete euphoria within me. I never realized how much I missed skin-to-skin contact until now. Or maybe I never missed it at all until he came into my life.

He continues his descent, worshipping my naked body. And that's exactly how it feels. Like he is worshipping me with his hands, his mouth, and his tongue.

"I'm going to taste this sweet pussy, but I've got all night to do that. Right now, I need to be inside you."

He reaches for the condom he tossed on the bed earlier, ripping it open and sliding it down his impressive length. Hands on my knees, he spreads me wide as he lines up to my opening. My eyes are glued to where my body waits for him.

"Eyes on me, Bebe. I want to see you as you take every inch of me."

When I snap my eyes to his, he starts to slide inside. Slowly. Deliciously slowly as my body opens and accepts him. Adjusts to his size. Molds around him. Welcomes the pressure of having him within me. Fuck, that's good. I forgot how good.

"You okay?" he asks.

"So, so good."

And that's all he needs to hear as he slowly pulls out before pushing back in. Rhythmically. Slowly. Too slowly.

"Faster," I encourage.

The expression on his face shifts, and he knows I'm fine. I can take it, and, more importantly, I want it.

His pace increases and he leans forward, placing his left hand by my hip while using his right to lift my knees, spreading me even wider. He plunges deeper, hitting the perfect spot within.

"Right. There," I huff out in staccato to match his pace. I brace myself by grabbing his right bicep with my left hand and a firm hold to his ass with the other, encouraging him to give it to me harder.

He continues to pound into me, my body willingly taking all he has to give. His right hand comes to my clit, matching the rhythm of his thrusts, providing the extra stimulation I need to fall over the edge. My back arching, his mouth finds my nipple as he sucks hard, shooting another jolt of pleasure right to my core. I scream his name as I come, not caring at all that my teammates may very well hear.

One, two, three more thrusts, and Griff is following me over. His body stiff, he plants himself hard, buries his face in my neck, and groans out his release.

We lay there for a few moments, the sound of our heavy breathing filling the air, my hand leaving his ass to rub lazily up and down his muscular back.

"I should take care of the condom," he says into the side of my neck. "But fuck if I want to move."

"It's fine for another minute," I reply. Because I don't want to move just yet either. I want to soak up every second of this moment.

"I could get used to hearing you scream my name," he says as he lifts his head to make eye contact.

"Funny, because I could get used to screaming it," I respond with a laugh, leaning forward to drop a quick kiss on his full lips.

CHAPTER 18

Griffin

I WASN'T ACTIVELY looking for a relationship.

A woman.

Anything.

Just trying to do my job and do it well.

The complication of Bebe Grimshaw wasn't welcome at first. That first night I stalked her and saw her through her kitchen window, I was pissed Bogachev had laid this on my doorstep. Yet, I wasn't going to turn my back on this strange woman who was now in extreme danger.

She was so fucking beautiful and mysterious. I had no clue that in just shy of two weeks, I'd be lying naked in her bed.

Bebe doesn't sleep well. She tosses and turns, startling easy. I would think someone who probably slept for shit for so many years in prison would sleep like the dead now, but she doesn't.

Lying on my side facing her, I hold still and just watch her. Her facial features are smoothed out, lips slightly parted as she breathes shallowly, probably just floating on the edge of consciousness. The sheet is pulled up over her breasts, but I take a moment to admire some of the artwork she has on her arms and shoulders. Her tattoos are nowhere near as prolific as mine, which bleed into each other and tell a moving story. Bebe's are individualized, perhaps denoting just brief moments in her life.

I hope there comes a day when I can learn about those moments. All of them. The ones when she was just a brilliant college student, those where she was lulled into crime, and those where she did her penance. I want to know it all.

But for now, I'll take what she's giving me, which is her body and little bits of insight into her soul as she allows.

Reaching out, I trail a finger over Bebe's collarbone. As expected, the barely-there touch causes her to wake up. Her eyes don't even flutter, but merely pop wide open. She slowly rolls her head on the pillow, giving me a languid smile.

"Good morning." Pushing up onto an elbow, I move my finger from her collarbone, down her chest, and hook it into the edge of the sheet. I start to drag it over her breasts, her nipples contracting hard when they're revealed.

"Good morning," she replies, her voice smoky and inviting.

I lean over, bringing my mouth to hers to experience our first morning kiss together. Bebe isn't shy. Her arms wrap around my neck, and she draws me down.

My body instantly reacts, despite the fact it should be well sated. We went at it all night, and I have to believe Bebe might be a little sore.

Reluctantly, I pull my lips from hers. Her eyes are half-closed, her lips puffy and I wait for her to focus in on me. "How are you feeling this morning?"

Bebe shifts, gives a little moan, and admits. "Like I had a lot of sex last night."

Chuckling, I press my mouth to hers for a hard, swift kiss. "How about a hot bath?"

Her lips purse into the cutest pout. "No bathtub in the little apartment."

"Hot shower?" I offer instead.

She seems to consider that, but then gives me a sly smile. "Admittedly, I'm a bit sore, but I'm also not afraid of a little pain."

I cock an eyebrow.

"Besides," she says almost coyly, but it's a direct challenge if I ever heard one. "Your mouth is super soft, or so I seem to remember."

She should fucking remember. I made her come at least three times by my count with my face between her legs.

My voice is gruff, completely turned on by the fact

she wants it. That this woman, who has every reason to be insecure in bed given her history, is requesting for me to give her pleasure. I fucking love it. "I can totally make that happen for you, beautiful girl."

Bebe blushes, bringing her hand to my face. She caresses my cheek, running her fingertips through my beard to clasp onto my chin before she pulls me back down for another kiss.

A shrieking sound emits from Bebe's phone on the nightstand, the alarm so shrill it causes me to jolt.

"Shit," Bebe mutters, rolling away from me to grab her phone. She taps the screen a few times, then her eyes start moving back and forth as she reads something I can't quite make out over her shoulder. "Goddamn it."

"What's wrong?" I ask, on high alert as I roll out of the bed and start searching for my jeans.

She twists to me, opens her mouth to say something, but then just freezes. Her eyes start roaming over my body, her eyes filling with appreciation and hunger. Just having her gaze on me like that causes my dick to twitch and lengthen.

I stand there, letting her have her fill. When she pins her eyes on my cock, I have to physically restrain myself from lunging.

Gently, I try to bring her back to reality as that alarm on her phone sounded urgent. "Bebe… what was that on your phone?"

She blinks slowly, then shakes her head. Her eyes clear, and the lust is replaced with concern. "It's um… well, Saint… you remember meeting him, right?"

I nod.

"Well, a few months ago, he broke up a huge heist ring in Paris, but the bad guy sort of got away. I've deployed some facial recognition software out to some airport security feeds to see if I can find him and—"

"Wait a minute." My hand goes up as my brow furrows. "What do you mean you deployed software?"

She flushes with guilt, and I hold my hand up again.

"Never mind," I quickly say. "Don't tell me."

If she's doing something illegal, she most definitely cannot tell me as I'm still an FBI agent and would be duty-bound to do something about it.

"At any rate," she says slowly, as if measuring every word before it comes out. "He's been spotted in Antigua."

"The bad guy?"

"Yup," she replies as she rises and heads into the small bathroom. "And I need to let Saint know. This man probably has a vendetta against him, and—"

"You need to alert the authorities," I say as I follow her in, trying hard not to get sidetracked by what a great ass she has or the beautiful angel wings she has tattooed on her shoulders.

Bebe reaches into the shower to turn the water on. "I

can't do that."

"Why not?"

"Can't tell you that," she mutters.

"Can't or won't?" I press.

"Can't," she confirms, but then adds, "But also won't. I'm sorry, Griff. But you're a federal law enforcement officer. While we're the good guys here at Jameson, sometimes we do things a little outside of the rules if you know what I mean."

"I'm starting to get that," I murmur uneasily, rubbing at the back of my neck. "You know we can't do anything that breaks the law while taking Bogachev down, right?"

"I realize that," she replies without flinching. "Which is why I'm glad you're here, so you can help me navigate around what's kosher and what's not."

It's in this moment I realize how tricky enlisting Jameson's help on my case could be. One tiny little thing that breaches the law could jeopardize years of work I've spent to bring down an incredibly dangerous criminal.

For another moment, I have some doubt about whether this is the right way to go about things. But then again, Bebe is brilliant. No one in our division has been able to crack Bogachev, and she could be just the answer we need.

Or perhaps I'm selfishly wanting the time with her now that I know exactly how sweet she tastes.

Fuck.

"Listen," she says with good nature. "I'm not going to do anything you don't approve. I promise."

Of course I'll take her word for it. I have no reason not to trust her.

"Okay," I reply, putting my hands to her cheeks and leaning in to kiss her.

Her body moves into mine, her softness pressing in and touching all the right parts. I slide my hands from her face to her ass, holding her tightly. Her little moan sets me on fire, and my need to be inside of her is instantaneous.

When I pick Bebe up, her legs wrap around my waist, her warm pussy settling against my cock. "Let's go back to bed."

"Shower," she mutters with her mouth against mine.

"Not practical," I remind her. "Condoms in the other room."

Giggling, and with her lips fluttering over mine, she says, "You're so freaking smart."

"Not as smart as you," I say as I turn from the bathroom. When I reach the bed, I put one knee to the mattress and lower our bodies down.

It doesn't escape my notice that even though we aren't yet joined, every part of her fits against every part of me extremely well. That even goes beyond the physical. Bebe has become important to me in a short period of time, which makes it all the more imperative we take Bogachev down sooner rather than later.

He's not just a threat to Bebe's security anymore. He's a threat to my future happiness.

♦

I FOLLOW BEBE to the freight elevator. She's in work mode now, which is about a hundred and eighty degrees away from where she was just an hour ago when she was underneath me in the bed.

We made love and I was gentle with her, compensating from a night of being rough and fervent. I vow to leave her alone tonight, but I know I'm lying to myself if I think I can keep that promise. I'm already imagining it, and it vexes me because I've never had a woman take such hold of me before.

It helps though… that Bebe's back in professional mode. She has an urgency about her to get this done so she can get back to a normal life.

Of course, I have no clue where I might fit into her normal life, and that's not something I can afford to dwell on. Right now, as we work side by side during the day and spend our nights together, our bond is growing. When this case is over, I'll head back to D.C. where I'm based out of, and she'll continue her life here in Pittsburgh. Which implies this may only be a fling, but fuck if it feels like that.

We take the elevator down to the abandoned first floor, then move to a separate elevator that takes us down to the Research and Development area where Bebe works out of. I had thought it might look like something straight out of a James Bond movie, the subversive research and development division of British Secret Service with cinder block walls and concrete flooring. Bebe, of course, is the equivalent of Q, so I expected a basement filled with people conducting experiments with all kinds of cool gadgets.

Instead, I walk into a room that looks like it was pulled straight off the movie set of *Black Panther*. Bebe isn't Q, but rather T'Challa's younger and insanely brilliant sister, Shuri. Despite being stuck one level down below the earth's surface, her R&D facility is bright—almost luminescent. Gleaming white tile floors, glassed walls, and sleekly designed standing desks also in white with chrome detailing. The computer equipment is white, and it's so elegantly designed it looks almost alien. There's even a clear acrylic thought board where they've written out equations and design ideas in neon blue chalk ink. Long tables—all made of stainless steel—are parceled throughout the room. They look to hold various technology items. I see weapons, electronic devices, and other gadgets that I have no clue what they are used for.

Dozer is bent over one such table, tinkering with a black box he has cracked open that is filled with circuitry boards.

He glances up, giving us both a short but welcoming smile before going back to his task. Clearly, he's a multitasker because he talks to us as he works. "Morning. Been brewing an idea about how we can upgrade that USB stick Griff planted on Bogachev's TV."

"Yeah, sure," Bebe replies vaguely, moving over to what I assume is her desk. She presses a button on her desktop unit, and it starts to cold boot.

"What's wrong with you?" Dozer asks, his gaze now locked on her. It's a testament to how well he must know her, because he's deduced something's wrong just from her body language and the tone of the two words she uttered.

But I could also tell she was a bit withdrawn as we left her small apartment and headed down here.

"I found Mercier," she admits, and Dozer gives a low whistle of surprise.

"Where?" he asks.

"Antigua."

Mercier is clearly the man she had told me about a bit ago after the alarm on her phone went off. Bebe obviously doesn't care if I know the name, throwing it out there so freely to Dozer.

"Have you told Kynan and Saint?" Dozer asks.

"I sent them a text a bit ago." She cuts a look my way, clearly not wanting to say much in front of my

Fibbie ears. "So they may want to call a meeting on that this morning."

Dozer nods. "I'm sure Kynan will want me to map out some different scenarios and probabilities."

"And then we'll have to manage Saint," Bebe points out. "He's more apt to run off after Mercier and take care of the problem himself."

"Nah," Dozer says with a chuckle. "He's not going to do something stupid, not when Sin's got a bun in the oven."

I swivel back and forth between them as they talk out their problem, but I'm only following about half of it. But as interesting as the issue is, I'm sidetracked by something else. "Saint? Sin? Those are their real names? Seriously?"

Bebe smirks. "Yup."

I shake my head, refocusing. "What's the risk to Saint?"

Dozer gives me an apologetic smile. "Sorry, man. See... Saint infiltrated an organization that was planning a huge heist—"

"Dozer," Bebe says in warning.

She gets an eyeroll in return. "Relax... I'm not going to tell Griff about any of the hundreds of ways we might have broken international laws to bring this guy down."

Bebe groans, putting her face in the palms of her hands. Laughing, I nod at Dozer. "Yeah... don't tell me those details. But tell me what you can, and maybe I can help."

It's Bebe who fills me in. "It's really not a big deal. Nothing will probably come out of it. But let's just say Saint executed an ingenious plan that took this guy, Mercier, down for the largest diamond heist in history. The guy was arrested, but he managed to escape before he was brought to trial."

"And you think he poses a danger to Saint?" I ask.

Bebe shrugs. "Maybe. But maybe not. The man was filthy rich, and he has enough money to disappear forever."

I cross my arms over my chest. "Yet, he showed his face in Antigua. He can't be that scared he'll get caught."

"It's a catch twenty-two," Dozer says. "We use our technology to help him get captured and brought to justice, but the flip side is Saint could be at risk for getting in trouble for some of the things he did. Or we just let him continue his life on the run, knowing that as long as he's outside of custody, he won't drop the dime on the things he knows about Saint."

"But," I manage to conclude, finally understanding. "He might want to execute this vendetta against Saint, meaning he's at risk that way."

"Exactly," Bebe says, sighing so heavily her hair blows back from her forehead. "But… nothing we can do about that right now. It's going to take some talking things through with Saint, but that's for later. For right now, we need to start figuring out how to get the information Griff needs on Bogachev."

"Within the confines of the law," I add with a grin.

"If you insist," she drawls dramatically, shooting me a wink. She then nods at the acrylic thought board. "Dozer... you take point. Let's get to brainstorming."

The rest of the morning is spent tossing up ideas on the board, arguing them through and erasing those that won't work. Bebe and Dozer's brains coming together is an amazing thing to watch, and I'm basically providing the parameters in which they have to work.

At noon, I head out on my own to grab something to eat while Bebe and Dozer meet with Kynan and Saint to discuss this Mercier fellow. As I eat an Italian sub, I'm tempted to google this guy, but I ultimately decide against it.

I'm afraid I might learn something from a news article that could cause me to want to dig a little deeper, which could theoretically lead me to some damning conclusions against Bebe and the people here at Jameson.

And something I've come to learn very quickly... I like these guys. Despite their methods and the fact they don't mesh all that well with my duties as a law enforcement officer, I don't want to see a single one go down for their... *extreme methods.*

So instead, I give Aaron a call to see how things are

going. I talk to Gloria for a few moments too, mainly to assure her that Bebe is doing okay.

I next handle the unpleasant task of texting a fake update to Bogachev, telling him that I've got a promising lead in California and I'll update him in a few days. That should keep him off my back until then.

If we're lucky, we'll have a plan long before I'm obligated to give him another fake update and we can implement a takedown of the bastard.

CHAPTER 19

Bebe

M
Y APARTMENT DOOR opens. Griff comes in
looking completely out of place, leading the little
four-pound Yorkie by the leash.

This is the weekend I told Dozer I'd watch Brutus so
he could do a weekend getaway in Miami with his
current flavor. Ordinarily, I'd just stay at Dozer's place
for convenience as he has a tiny fenced-in yard. I have to
say it's much nicer dog sitting while being able to open
the back door for him to go out and do his business
versus having to walk him on the city streets.

Staying at Dozer's, however, was not an option as a
Russian mobster and cybercriminal wants me dead.
Although there are no indications Bogachev thinks I'm
still alive, no one wants to take any chances. Thus, Dozer
dropped Brutus off with two days' worth of food and
treats, as well as poop bags and sincere apologies we'd
have to pick up his shit when we walked him.

Well… when Griffin walked him. He gallantly offered to do it, also preferring to keep me safe behind

Jameson doors.

"Who's the goodest little pupper ever?" Griff exclaims in a baby voice to Brutus, who bounces around his ankles over the attention. "Who went poopy and pee-pee like a good little boy?"

I stare at Griff, blinking over his antics. He sheepishly grins at me.

"What?" he asks.

Shaking my head, I turn back to emptying the dishwasher. "There are many attractive things about you. Your build. Your brawn. Your long hair and tatts. You're a total badass on your Harley. But you talking to that little dog like that pretty much ensures you're not going to get laid tonight."

Griff snorts as he unclips the leash from Brutus' collar. The little dog runs over to the couch, then makes quite the athletic leap onto the cushions. He spins around three times, plops down, and puts his head on his paws before shutting his eyes.

"Laugh all you want," he says with a somber nod. "But that dog practically pees and poops on command if you talk to him that way. Dozer trained him well."

I can't help but laugh. "Knowing Dozer, he probably read a dozen research articles on house training dogs, developed his own protocol, conducted experiments, and solidified the 'baby talk' method."

"He should patent it," Griff remarks as he stands on

the other side of the small kitchen counter that separates the kitchen and living area. While the apartments Kynan had built on the fourth floor are luxuriously appointed with crown molding, hardwood floors, and high-end fixtures, they are small and efficiently spaced.

I continue to unload the dishwasher, intent on stacking it with our breakfast dishes. Griff treated me to homemade French toast after we woke up this morning, so the least I can do is clean.

"I want to get Aaron a dog," I say as I place our coffee cups in the top rack. "I think kids should have animals, and well… it just seems he should have a dog."

"I had dogs growing up. The type that could go hiking over the farm and roughhouse with me. I wouldn't recommend a dog like Brutus for Aaron. Maybe a Golden Retriever or something."

I put the last of the silverware in the basket, then close up the dishwasher. Wiping my hands on a hand towel, I admit, "I just want his childhood to be the best, you know? I have so much to make up for."

Griff bends over the counter, resting his forearms on the granite and clasping his hands. His eyes hold mine with warm empathy. "Can I ask you a personal question?"

I move directly opposite him. "Sure."

"Why did you do it? Why get messed up with Bogachev?"

His tone holds no recrimination. He appears genuinely curious, as if he's trying to place the last few pieces of a puzzle.

"It was easy money," I reply with a slight shrug. "It was as simple as that. I was a struggling student with a baby and a disabled mother with diabetes. And at first, it was just enough money to keep food on the table and pay my tuition. But then the jobs got more complex and the money got better. I was hacking corporations, so I never felt like I was hurting people. It was a terrible illusion I'd let myself believe, and I just got deeper and deeper."

"You were too good at what you did," he guesses. "They weren't going to let you out."

Because, yes. That's the other element as to why I got in so deep. "Bogachev noticed me... my work. By the time I realized just how dangerous he was, I was in far too deep to get out by merely declining to work for him. I was so stupid."

"You were so young, Bebe," Griff says, the compassion in his voice settling over me like a warm blanket. It took me a long time not to immediately discount such empathy.

I shrug again, nabbing the hand towel to wipe off nonexistent crumbs from the counter.

"And brave," Griff continues. His words startle me, and I snap my eyes up to lock with his.

"Brave?"

"I read your file," he says without apology. "Kynan filled me in on some of it. Bogachev forced you to steal nuclear codes, and you couldn't put your country at risk. You got yourself caught, so the codes would stay safe."

"And Aaron." I give him a weak smile. "I kept my mouth shut and went to prison to keep Aaron safe."

"So very brave," he reiterates with a soft smile, reaching across the counter and taking my hand in his.

"I don't feel like it was enough to pay for my mistakes," I admit.

Griff scoffs. "Seven years in prison without your kid? You kept your country safe. You more than paid for it. I'm telling you, you need to let that go. Your family and friends have. I don't care what you did then—I only care about the person you are today. So quit being so hard on yourself."

I squeeze his hand, my smile a little stronger. I know he's right. If I had a nickel for every time I heard that from one of my friends—Kynan, Dozer, Saint, Cruce, Joslyn, and Anna.

Even Aaron. My wise little boy knows the entire story, and he's told me the same.

Let it go.

Griff lifts our hands in the air, giving a tug to lead me around the counter until I come to stand directly in front of his big body. He returned from New York four days ago, and he's been staying with me at the Jameson apartment since then. We've spent our days down in R&D, brainstorming and ultimately tinkering with my USB device we've simply dubbed The Hijacker, since we want it to capture Bogachev's network. We're going to be testing it out with Kynan and Joslyn tomorrow to see if it will do what I've created it to.

The nights, though, have been spent in my bed.

The couch.

Even the floor.

Wherever Griff decides to take me.

My sexual reawakening has been profound. Griff has done things to me—had me do things to him—that had never even crossed my mind. The years when I should have been experimenting with my lovers were wasted behind bars where access to penises was impossible.

I've made up for lost time. Griff lets me touch him all I want, taste all I need. He encourages me to explore. In return, he turns me inside out with his demanding ways. Sometimes, I find myself just staring at his body when he's asleep, memorizing the planes. I touch his skin as often as I can, noting the differences between his and mine. I've gotten over my early embarrassment about how much he loves his mouth between my legs. In turn, I've come to learn I love having his cock in my mouth.

I feel like springtime… like I'm waking up to a new dawn with endless possibilities.

"Come here," Griff murmurs in a low rumble. One more tug brings me flush against his body. His hands go to my hips, and he looks down solemnly. "I think you're amazing. Every bit of you. The part that was so smart you went to MIT to the part that was brazen enough to start hacking to make your way. You're an incredible mother. And, as a lover, you've rocked my world like no other."

His words thrill me. Settle me.

Just the way my skin tingles when he touches me, yet my soul feels quiet at the same time.

Griff renders me completely speechless, and his eyes sparkle with mischief because of it.

Hand squeezing my waist, he dips his head closer to mine. "We're testing out the Hijacker tomorrow morning. Any last-minute fiddles you need to make?"

I snort at his terminology. "I think what I do is a bit more complex than fiddling, but no… it's ready to go."

Lips curving upward, he nods. "So that means we have the rest of the day and the evening to ourselves?"

"That we do," I reply, my voice dropping to a husky level because I know where he's going with this. Then I amend with a grin. "Except seeing to Brutus' needs."

"He's good for several hours before he has to go out again or even eat," Griff points out.

"Which means we could say… just get naked for the rest of the day?"

"Oh, we can totally do that," he agrees before bringing his mouth down on mine. My hands go to his face, fingers stroking the softness of his beard. I wonder what he looks like underneath it, but not thinking I could love his face better without it. Really, with Griff... it's all about his eyes. They're so expressive in their green beauty I could just stare into them for hours.

Griff's lips turn from sweetly exploring to persistently demanding. His hands work at my shirt, tugging it up and over my head, breaking the kiss for mere seconds to get it off me. My bra follows, his large hands covering my breasts. He squeezes, rubbing the pads of his thumbs over my nipples. The sensation is so exquisite I start to make all sorts of unholy sounds deep within my throat.

Before long, my jeans are unzipped and Griff's hand is pushed into my panties. I'm drenched, his fingers filling me up. My clit pulses, and his first brush against it about brings me to my knees.

"So responsive," he praises, moving his mouth to my ear. "So beautiful and wet just for me."

I nod, practically riding his fingers he's got me so worked up. "Griff... let's go to the bedroom."

He chuckles, the sound causing a tremor to run up my spine. "Why would we do that when we have a perfectly good kitchen counter right here?"

Before I can even begin to understand his allusion, he's got me lifted up in his arms and my ass settled on the granite. His hands come to my jeans, and he starts to tug them down my hips. I have to lean back, plant my palms on the cool countertop, and lift my ass up so he can work.

They slide easily off over my bare feet. My panties follow, then his strong hand is on the center of my chest and he pushes me back. I slowly lower, glad for the wide counter, and flatten my back on it.

There's no guessing what he's about to do. Griff yanks my legs apart. As I stare at my kitchen ceiling, I feel his warm breath fan out over my inner thighs. He rubs his beard there a moment, the sensation ticklish and erotic at the same time.

Then that amazing mouth is on me, creating a vortex of sensations. He seems to be everywhere at once. Everything is so soft I can't tell where his mouth ends and his tongue begins.

All I know is my body reacts to him swiftly. It's clear he owns me. Every inch of me. And I'm okay with that ownership.

My pulse quickens, my breathing becomes erratic, and my sex is a throbbing, dripping mess of needful release.

Griff sucks hard on my clit, knowing exactly what I need without me having to say a word. I shatter with such violence tears leak out of my eyes, and I feel like I just experienced a religious event. How the man manages to drive me up so high, so fast, only to destroy me at the apex so I free fall with no care as to anything in the world is beyond me.

When my body is pulled from the counter, I'm as limp as a rag doll. Griff merely turns from the kitchen area to the sofa right behind us. He bends me over it, his hands warm on my backside.

"So fucking sexy," he murmurs, his fingers digging into my ass cheeks. In this moment, I know he's doing nothing more than staring at my naked body bent over with my ass tipped up in the air for his pleasure.

Cool air hits my skin when he removes his hands, but I hear the sound of a foil packet being opened and then his zipper coming down. My blood starts racing again, knowing that he's going to be filling me up soon.

His hands go back to my ass, then I feel the tip of him probing against my entrance. He's a big man, but not impossibly so. Still, I feel such a delicious stretch when he breeches me, slowly opening my flesh as it molds around him in invitation.

Griff groans as he pushes all the way inside me, his pelvis pressed against my ass. The zipper treads on his jeans bite lovingly into my skin, and who would have ever thought I'd enjoy a bit of pain with my sex?

This is something Griff and I discovered the other night, and there was a bit of spanking involved. If he wanted to let loose on me right now, I would not complain… but I would scream.

But he doesn't. Instead, he pulls his thick length out of me only to plunge back in ever so slowly. I can feel every amazing inch slide along my flesh.

Griff may have quickly thrown me over the back of the couch to fuck me, but he does it with such sweetness and deliberate motion it can't be considered anything but lovemaking. It goes on and on, Griff's motions building his own orgasm up. I listen to his ragged breathing.

The tiny grunts of pleasure he emits as he takes more and more of me.

Griff's hand comes to my jaw and he leans over me, driving in deep. He pulls me up a bit, forces my face around to look at him for what I think might be a kiss. Instead, he just stares, our noses almost touching while he holds himself still inside me.

"We need to figure this out," he murmurs in a liquid tone.

"Figure what out?"

"How we keep this going after it's all said and done," he replies simply before leaning in and giving me a soft kiss.

I get no chance to respond or come up with a solution. I don't even have the opportunity to think about how happy it makes me that he's even thinking of such a thing at a time like this.

Because he's fucking me again, slow and deep, and all I want to do right now is languish in the feel of him inside my body, knowing he's touched places inside of me no one ever has.

CHAPTER 20

Griffin

THE FIRST BETA test for Bebe's Hijacker is going down this afternoon, and the excitement between us is palpable. The science and brain work behind it is far too advanced for me to comprehend, but from what I understand, the USB device she had me plug into Bogachev's TV has a receptor board that will accept commands from her unique, encrypted signal. Theoretically, from that tiny receptor, she can take control of Bogachev's Wi-Fi and slip into his network that way.

The problem is in getting her signal to the USB device from hundreds of miles away here in Pittsburgh. As such, she had to do some complex coding that will sort of hopscotch along various Wi-Fi connections, all the way to New York. While Bebe was busy this week with said coding, my FBI colleagues were busy working with the justice department to get access warrants to the Wi-Fi portals between Pittsburgh and New York. The last bit of paperwork was finalized this morning, so we're testing this baby out.

It's a small test first. Something that should not be difficult at all for Bebe to crack. Kynan's going to the Fairmont Hotel in downtown Pittsburgh this afternoon, and he'll plug an identical USB stick into their TV system. This is all being done with the hotel's consent and with help from their own IT folks, but for the most part, they're allowing us to see if we can hack into their network this way.

Bebe and I headed east, taking a leisurely trip to the small town of Johnstown, Pennsylvania roughly sixty miles away. We're currently biding time in a great little restaurant called Press Bistro, enjoying a late lunch of grilled paninis and shooting the shit.

It's one of my favorite things to do with Bebe.

Not eating paninis, but just talking about anything and everything. Over the last several days, we've occupied ourselves plenty between the sheets, but we've spent more time just talking.

I've been staying at her apartment inside the Jameson building for almost seven days. That's almost a hundred and sixty-eight hours together, not taking into account the time spent sleeping. But I count it because even in sleep, we communicate. It's in the way Bebe moves effortlessly into my embrace just before we shut our eyes, a strong indication of trust and bonding. She spent years alone without anyone to hold her, and I'm still amazed at the ease with which she gives herself over to me.

It's communication.

In those moments, when she lets me hold her all night, it's as if she says, "Griff... you're my person. I'm depending on you to keep me secure through the night. I know you won't let me down."

She'd be right about that too.

Bebe studies her phone. "Kynan says everything's in place. Are you about ready to go?"

I look down at my empty plate with my used napkin tossed on top. I had finished eating a good twenty minutes ago, but we've been biding our time, waiting for Kynan's go ahead.

"Yeah... ready," I say, scoping the room to locate our waitress. She's at a nearby table, and we make eye contact. Lifting my chin, I mouth for her to bring our check. I get a cheery smile in return.

I settle back into the booth to wait, watching Bebe with a smile. She has her laptop on the table, diligently pounding out whatever smarty-pants shit is in her brain. She amazes me.

Her brow furrows in concentration, her tongue peeking out the side of her mouth. It's fucking adorable.

Eyes lifting, she gives me a lopsided grin. "Stop staring."

"Nothing else to do," I point out. "Plus... I like the view."

She shakes her head and laughs, tapping on her keyboard. "I'm sorry I'm ignoring you. Just sending out a quick email to Dozer on an idea I had for another project."

"Does your brain ever stop coming up with new ideas?" The awe in my voice is evident because she blushes.

"Not really," she admits, shutting her laptop and giving me her full attention. "Weird?"

"Sexy," I reply with a wink.

"Yeah, right," she scoffs, then reaches for her water to take a sip. The waitress comes to the table and I snag the bill, reaching for my wallet. She waits while I pull out my wallet, nabbing a twenty and a ten to hand to her. "Keep the change."

"Thank you," she exclaims.

When the waitress meanders off, Bebe says, "Hey... did I tell you Saint decided not to go after Mercier?"

She hadn't, and I purposely have not asked. I'm well aware Bebe's work on that case probably ran afoul of some laws—both international and domestic—and I don't want to know a damn thing about it. I cannot be put in a position where I have to keep my duty to my country and my loyalty to Bebe, which she now definitely has, separate.

I don't respond, but give a hesitant shake of my head. She gives me a soft smile in understanding. Her words are carefully chosen. "He had a pretty lengthy talk with his fiancée, Sin. They're both pretty confident Mercier's not going to do anything to jeopardize his own freedom, so it's doubtful he'd come after them. Still, they're going to be extra cautious for a while. I'll just keep an eye…"

Her words trail off as she realizes she's starting to say too much. The mere fact she's keeping an eye on a fugitive implies she has some serious hacking going on that's probably not legal, and I choose to ignore what she might have revealed had she kept going on.

"It's funny," she says, dropping her gaze down to the table. "We're both doing work for the good guys. On essentially the same side, and yet… we're still miles apart in how we ethically carry out our jobs."

"Which is why your shit should stay mostly top-secret," I remind her.

"It sucks," she says plainly. "I don't like keeping things from you."

Maybe months or years later, I'll look back on this conversation and won't give it much credence, but for right now, her words are pretty impactful. It makes it clear just how close the two of us have grown in just a few weeks' time.

Moreover, for the first time since I became a Fed, I sort of wish I wasn't. My job is negatively impacting a positive relationship I have going on, and I don't like it. I expect as we continue to progress, we're going to have to set up some stringent boundaries that will keep parts of our lives removed from the other.

Bebe and I slide out of the booth, then head out into the crisp fall air of western Pennsylvania. Within the next week or so, the leaves are going to be at their peak color change. I'm thinking a drive back through this area with Bebe would be a nice way to spend the day.

Except, fuck if I know where we'll be then.

We make our way over to the rental car, which I'd parked several blocks down. After I unlock the doors, I slip into the driver's seat. Bebe gets in the passenger seat, pulling out her laptop and booting it back up.

Surfing my phone, I wait patiently while she does her thing. I scroll through my texts, particularly to the one I received from Bogachev yesterday asking for an update. I'd responded fairly quickly with another benign statement saying I was still searching for Bebe's son and mother. His response came back just as quickly, but it had me slightly puzzled.

Bogachev is a paranoid control freak. Any job not getting done as quickly as possible always drives him crazy. He'll rant and threaten, constantly trying to drive a mission's conclusion through sheer will when he really can't do a damn thing to make it go faster. It's irritating, to say the least.

However, when he replied, it was merely to say, *Just keep me updated.*

Now, that could mean several things. It could simply be he's busy with something else, and he didn't have time to rant. It could be that with the elimination of Bebe—his main threat—he's not overly worried about her family members.

Or, worst case, it could mean he's on to me and knows I'm not working for him at all. I can never discount that as a potential option, so I must always proceed forward with the thought Bogachev is as much a danger to me as he is to Bebe.

Regardless, nothing to be done about it now. We are moving forward with our plan to let Bebe hack his network and get the mirror-image data we need so we can effectuate arrest warrants.

Bebe starts clacking away on her keyboard. She pauses, then reaches into her bag on the floorboard and pulls out a device about the size of a USB drive. It, in fact, has a USB plug and a stubby little antenna on the end. After plugging it into the side of her laptop, she starts typing again.

"Can you get Kynan on the phone?" she asks without missing a beat on her keyboard. "I'm about ready to deploy."

I dial Kynan, getting him on speakerphone. "I'm in their IT room with their head guy," he explains. "The device is in one of the hotel rooms. We're ready on our end."

"Just doing one more thing," Bebe mutters, more to herself than for Kynan's benefit. She spends a few more minutes with her fingers flying over the keyboard before she stops, her eyes locking onto me. "Okay… it's ready."

I smile, and her return one is a little hesitant but not without hope. Reaching out, I glide my knuckles over her cheekbone, my silent moment of solidarity with her.

She leans into me. Eyes closing halfway, she allows herself just a second or two to cherish my touch. Then she turns her attention back to her laptop and depresses the Enter key.

"I've deployed the code," she says. There's silence on Kynan's end. I suspect they're hunched over the equipment in the Fairmont's IT room, waiting to see if our test hack is successful.

We both hold our breaths as several long moments pass by.

Finally, Bebe asks, "Are you seeing anything on your end?"

"Nothing," Kynan replies.

She mutters a curse, then starts working on the laptop again, her expression frustrated.

"Shit," she exclaims, leaning in closer to her screen.

"What is it?" Kynan asks.

"I was able to lock onto the first Wi-Fi port, but the signal's not jumping to the next one. It's just too weak, and that could be for any number of reasons."

"Let's just wait a bit," I suggest, eyes scanning the sequence of numbers and words on her screen that look like a foreign language to me.

So we do.

For another fifteen minutes, with Bebe becoming more and more frustrated.

"It's not working," she snarls, slamming back into the car seat. My chest aches when I see a slight sheen in her eyes.

"Break it down for me, Bebe," Kynan says over the line. "What's the problem?"

She huffs, shaking her head. "It's just too unpredictable. In different circumstances, the feed might be better. It might not. I've got everything correct on my end. The Wi-Fi ports are open for us to access. It's just an instability from point A to point B."

That makes slightly more sense to me.

"So we try again at a different time," Kynan suggests.

"Or we just fucking go to New York, park our car outside his apartment building, and let me hack him there. The signal will be strong enough at that point."

"No," Kynan and I exclaim at the same time.

"You are not getting anywhere near Bogachev," I say with a hard shake of my head.

"Agreed," Kynan says.

Bebe narrows her eyes, her jaw locking tight. Through gritted teeth, she says in a frost-covered tone,

"You're not the boss of me, Griff."

"But I am," Kynan says quietly, but his words reverberate throughout the car. "And we're just going to have to figure out something else."

"That's not—" Bebe starts to say.

"Get back to Pittsburgh," Kynan orders, and there's no leniency in his command. "We'll have to regroup and figure out something else. Or the FBI can just go it alone again, but, either way, you're not going to New York."

The line goes dead, Kynan having clearly disconnected the call.

Wincing, I survey Bebe. Although I can't hear her, I can see her lips move and read exactly what she says.

I am so going to New York.

CHAPTER 21

Bebe

G RIFF CASTS A worried glance from across the room. My return look is sullen as I listen to Sin updating Joslyn on her pregnancy. She's three and a half months along.

Roles are reversed tonight. The women are in the living area, sipping at drinks and nibbling on appetizers, while the men are in the kitchen putting dinner together. Kynan organized this little get-together to be held once a month for anyone from Jameson who wants to attend. Some nights, we barely have room to move around the communal living area and kitchen. Other times, like tonight, it's a bit more intimate with only a handful of people.

I take in the men of Jameson where they are gathered around the kitchen island, swilling their beers while they talk about football and hunting season. They decided to make pizza, and they're haphazardly throwing toppings on the four large crusts laid out along the counter.

Griff has fallen right into the ranks, lately bonding

with Dozer, who is fresh off his hot date with some woman in Miami. Saint and Cruce rib Kynan for putting pineapple and ham on a pizza.

As for the women, we're sprawled around the living room. Sin and Joslyn have the couch, while Barrett is in one of the comfy chairs with her legs crossed and a glass of wine. She's listening to Sin and Joslyn, sometimes looking over to me in the chair opposite her. She always quickly averts her eyes, and I'm sure it's because of the sour expression I've been wearing all night.

I look back to Griff to find him still staring. He's taken the brunt of my frustration as I've spent all day railing at him because I want to go to New York and end Bogachev's reign of criminality.

Of course, I'm well aware it's not actually Griff keeping me from this task, but rather Kynan. After all, he is my boss, and he's simply refusing to let me go.

To give Griff credit, he's strangely been on my side.

Kind of.

I mean, in the car on the return trip to Pittsburgh from Johnstown, he spent a lot of time explaining how he didn't think it was wise for me to go to New York. It had to do with my personal safety and how, despite New York being a city of over eight million people, he's worried about Bogachev getting his hands on me.

We both know it's ridiculous to think I'd be spotted. Precautions would be taken so I could get close enough to hack Bogachev's system without being noticed. But Griff is concerned over the slight possibility Bogachev knows I'm still alive. Has somehow doubted Griff all along and has figured things out.

While unlikely, it's his main dislike of my suggestion that we just go and get this done.

Over the rest of the day, I've worn him down a bit. I've methodically pled my case, including all the ways in which we could ensure my safety.

"Hell," I told him as we sat on opposite ends of my couch, sipping on beers. "Surround me with a fucking SWAT team for all I care."

Ultimately, Griff had to agree that it was possible to keep me relatively safe, but we still had the stumbling block of a man named Kynan who wouldn't approve of me going.

By the time we meandered out of my apartment to join the get-together in the common area, I'd still been hell-bent on convincing Kynan to let me go. If I'm not successful in doing so, Griff is going to have to head back to New York and put himself under Bogachev's notice until he can figure out another way to get the data. That puts Griff's life at unnecessary risk, and I'm strongly averse to that, as one could imagine.

"Okay, pizzas are going in," Kynan announces. Good thing he upfitted our communal kitchen with two commercial-grade double ovens.

"About time," Joslyn calls. "We're about to perish from starvation."

"Please, woman," Kynan retorts to his wife. "Have another glass of wine."

The women laugh. All except me.

Griff gives me an understanding smile. I want to just go to my apartment and fume in privacy, but admittedly, I'm hungry. Besides, it seems petulant and I can't afford to have Kynan viewing me that way. I need him to take me seriously, because I have no intention of giving up my fight to get him to change his mind.

The freight elevator makes a hissing sound as it comes to a grinding stop, and everyone turns that way. Anna stands behind the scrolled rolling gate, which she opens before stepping out.

"You're late," Cruce exclaims with a grin. "Want a beer?"

"Sorry," she exclaims without smiling back. She moves toward the kitchen island, shakes her head at Cruce, and heads straight for Kynan. "I was finishing up the afternoon mail when this came in. I knew you'd want to see it as it might help Malik."

That gets everyone's attention. The women spring from their seats in the living area and hurry into the kitchen, closing in around the counter as Kynan opens the top flap.

As he pulls out the contents, Anna explains, "It's a

letter from a woman named Willow Monahan. She's a photographer who was with our guys just before they got ambushed. She just wanted to reach out to let us know she was there. She'd been interviewed by the government and has been thinking we'd reach out to her, but since we hadn't, she wanted to send the pictures."

"Pictures?" Cruce asks as he hands her the beer he'd pulled from the fridge.

Anna nods toward the stack of items Kynan just pulled free. Her expression darkens, and her voice trembles. "Photos she'd taken around their camp right before the ambush."

Without thought, I move immediately to Anna's side and put my arm around her shoulder. Her husband, Jimmy, was there, and I'm assuming there are photos of him. She trembles under my touch, and I can only imagine how difficult this is for her. She's trying so hard to be cool and collected as an employee of Jameson, but she just opened up an envelope and saw photos of her dead husband... perhaps the last taken before he was killed.

Kynan flips through the photos, a muscle in his jaw ticking as he does so. We all stand absolutely still and quiet except for Anna, who starts to nibble at one of her nails.

"Miss Monahan thought we might want to talk to her... ask questions. She heard the ambush and was fortunate to escape, but…"

Kynan nods, giving Anna a quick smile of comfort. "We'll absolutely want to talk to her. Maybe she'll have something that can give us a lead."

Anna swallows hard, giving a subtle nod. I pull her to me, giving a squeeze of reassurance. She knows our focus is on finding Malik, yet this is tearing open her wounds over losing Jimmy again.

Kynan puts the photos back into the manila envelope instead of passing them around. Even though I want to see them—have one last look at Jimmy and Sal and definitely want to see Malik, who we still hope beyond hope is alive—now is not the time.

"I'm sorry, Anna," Kynan says as he places the envelope on the counter. I step aside when Kynan strides over and puts his hands on her shoulders. "I know this is hard for you. Would you like to take a few days off—"

"No," Anna exclaims, her tone both pleading and hard at the same time. She lowers her voice a tad. "No, thank you. I love my job. Love being part of this team, and I love we're still looking for Malik. Being involved in this makes what happened to Jimmy almost bearable. He believed in his job and so do I, no matter the pain or risk to my heart."

No one says a word, although our hearts are clearly heavy with sympathy. Anna gives a cough to clear her throat, leveling Kynan with a bright smile. "As it stands,

I've actually got to get going so I can pick Avery up at my mom's."

"Stay and have pizza with us," Joslyn pleads, her expression conveying she doesn't believe for a moment Anna is as strong as she's trying to portray.

But as I study her, taking in the stubborn tilt to her chin and the clarity in her eyes, I actually think she's strong as fuck.

"I really can't," she says to Joslyn, giving a confident smile. "But I'm definitely in on next month's dinner."

She turns my way, giving me a much quieter smile, which I have a hard time returning. Anna nods before pivoting on her heel, then makes her way back to the elevator. We wave as she starts to descend out of sight. When she's gone, I spin on Kynan.

"Why do you let Anna take risks but not me?" I demand.

Immediately, I feel Griff move closer to me, a clear sign of solidarity. My words are taking him as much by surprise as Kynan, judging by the look on his face, but I'm sure Griff understands where I'm going with this.

Kynan cocks an eyebrow.

"She just told you that she knows the risks to her heart by working here at Jameson, given what happened to Jimmy," I explain, very aware that calling him out like this in front of everyone is probably not cool. Griff's arm goes around my waist, and he squeezes. "And you let her do it. So I want to know why, when it's me offering to take risks, you won't let me."

"Not the same thing," Kynan says in a low, warning tone. "You're talking risks to her heart, but with you… we're talking about a risk to your *life*."

I glare at Kynan. "And yet, you let Cruce, Saint, and Cage take risks with their lives all the time."

Kynan flushes beet red over that assertion. I'm calling out the double standard, yet he still has a response to it. "They are trained for their missions. They have special skills—"

"Then protect me," I snarl. "It's not that difficult, and I just need to get within a block or so of his apartment. Jesus… why can't you let me do this so I can get my damn life back?"

"Bebe," Kynan murmurs, apology written all over his face, but he's clearly not moved.

A wash of emotion comes over me, then I get hyperfocused on my situation. I've only felt this way one other time in my life, and I remember it with crystal clarity.

It was the moment I decided to let myself get caught by the U.S. government when I stole the nuclear codes— when I decided to sacrifice myself for my son's safety and welfare.

It blankets me with a soothing calm I very much need now, because I have to get my life back.

Raising an arm, I point a steadfast finger at Kynan.

"You send me to New York and let me see this to completion… or I quit."

Griff's fingers jerk against my waist. Kynan's eyes flare with surprise, even as his jaw locks down in clear anger over my demand. We stare at each other, both having drawn a very deep line the other doesn't want to cross. It's so quiet you could hear a pin drop and I wonder, no matter what happens after this, if I have just irrevocably ruined my good relationship with Kynan by giving him this ultimatum.

Finally, he gives me a curt nod. "Fine. You can go."

My body feels like it might collapse against Griff in pure relief, and I flash Kynan a brilliant and wide grin. "It will be fine. I promise. We'll get in, get it knocked out, and…"

My words die off as Kynan marches around the counter, moves right past me and Griff without even acknowledging me, and stomps down the stairs.

I whip my head toward Joslyn, because she knows him better than anyone and I need to know how badly I just fucked up my relationship with the man.

Pursing her lips, she gives me a slight shrug before moving off after her husband. We all watch her start down the stairs until she's out of sight, the silence becoming awkward.

Then the buzzer on the oven goes off, startling us.

"Pizza's ready," Dozer says with a laugh, grabbing a

pair of oven mitts from the counter.

I tip my head up to see Griff. He regards me thoughtfully, finally giving me a smile as he pulls me into his body. Leaning down, he presses his lips on my head and whispers. "Way to stand up for yourself."

"I'll be safe." It's the assurance Kynan needs, but I give it to Griff in his stead.

"Damn right you will," he replies gruffly. "Because I'm going to be right there with you."

I laugh as I wrap my arms around his waist, finally feeling like there's some light at the end of the tunnel. "Damn right you will."

CHAPTER 22

Griffin

THIS EARLY MORNING meeting with my FBI liaison, Ken Battersham, is the last bit of prep work we need to do before we make our move on Bogachev. We're meeting in a hotel room in midtown, just a few blocks from the hotel Bebe and I checked into late last night. We'd made the roughly six-hour drive from Pittsburgh to New York after spending most of the day at Jameson so Bebe and Dozer could fine-tune the Hijacker for our close-proximity use.

Kynan did a lot of hovering yesterday, demanding to know details. In general, he was being overbearing and obnoxious. He's still not happy Bebe threatened to quit if he didn't let her go, and he's probably even more unhappy with himself for giving in to her.

I figured it out though.

While Kynan isn't but eight years older than Bebe, he's very much a father to her. I never noticed it until they butted heads night before last because of his overprotectiveness, but then it became clear to me. He's worried for her on a personal level that surpasses that of a boss, and I have to give him credit for it. Ultimately, I had to give him a ton of reassurances we'd be safe and secure throughout.

At one point, he'd actually pulled me out of R&D and demanded to know, "How could you just roll over and support her doing this?"

My question back to him caught him off guard. "How can I not? Yes, she wants to get her life back so she's impatient, but it's more than that, Kynan. She wants an active role in taking Bogachev down. He's the one who ruined her life. If I had to guess, part of this is about revenge and vindication."

I'm not sure why those words made such an impact on him, but Kynan physically jolted when I said it. His brow furrowed and, if possible, he looked even more worried for Bebe.

Then… he just accepted it.

It was like night and day. After that, he got on board and was supportive. Bebe didn't notice the change because she was hyper-focused on her work, but I sure did.

When we got to the hotel last night, she had a hard time settling down to go to sleep. I had thought a couple of orgasms would help her out, but she was too wired. She tossed and turned all night just from knowing we're getting closer to the end. She finally fell asleep close to dawn, so when my alarm went off, I quickly shut it off and quietly slipped out of bed to dress in the dark. I wrote a quick note using the hotel stationary saying I'd be back soon with breakfast in case she does wake up.

It's not crucial she make this meeting because it's just to confirm locations and times. Ken's going to be our backup in case something goes sideways.

I knock on the hotel room door, and Ken opens it up within moments. He's about my age, and he has, so far, been good to work with on this case. We spent some time yesterday on the phone doing basic planning.

We shake hands, and I follow him in. We decided on a hotel room rather than meeting at the federal building, just to help keep my cover intact until the last possible moment. It's not going to be long now until I stop being Griffin Stoltz and become my real self of Griffin Moore.

Ken moves over to the table by the window, gesturing to a pot of coffee he has there along with two cups. I help myself to the caffeine before I sit down opposite him.

Pulling out a map that's been folded to focus in on a specific geographic location, he places it on the table facing me. I immediately recognize the streets of the Brooklyn neighborhood where Bogachev lives.

"How close does Bebe need to be to his building?" he asks.

These are schematics we'd already gone over in Pittsburgh yesterday, so I point to an area just south of Bogachev's high rise. "Two blocks. Figured we could park somewhere in this area."

"We've got the van requisitioned, and you can pick it up first thing in the morning," he says. "Just text me when you're ready, and I'll bring it over your way."

Ken obtained a city public works van that will allow us to park on the side of the street within viewing distance of Bogachev's building. The local police precincts will be aware it's an FBI operation and will leave us alone.

Because I know the area well, I point to another place on the map. "There's a cafe right here. They have a meal counter that runs along the windows. Get a seat there, and you'll have an unfettered view of us."

"That's a lot of distance between me and you if something goes wrong and you need my help," he remarks.

"Nothing's going to go wrong," I assure him. "Chances of Bogachev being on to us are very slim."

"But still—"

"You'll be right across the street and down half a block," I remind him soothingly. "It will be fine."

It better be fine. I'm not worried about myself, but Bebe will be there. I'd never be able to live with myself if something were to happen to her, yet I can't stand in her way of wanting to do this. I just know deep in my gut she wants to be the one to ultimately take him down or she'll never have the closure she wants.

No, *needs*.

And deserves.

Ken moves on, understanding the plan is already set. "Once you complete the mirror-image capture, I'll join you and we'll drive straight to the federal building to turn it in."

"My team in D.C. will be waiting for us to send it to them." We'll upload the data through a secure, encrypted server here at the local FBI office, and the cyber team in D.C. is on standby to go through it. We also have a federal attorney there who will be reviewing the evidence in real-time and ready to move.

Still, it will probably take a few days to get through it with enough detail to ensure the arrest warrants are tight. As soon as we upload the data, I intend to drive Bebe straight back to Pittsburgh, where we'll wait for confirmation of Bogachev's arrest. Only then will we feel comfortable getting Aaron and Gloria back to us.

"You sure you don't want in on the arrest?" Ken asks. We've already decided he and his team will be the ones to carry it out. "You've been working this for a long damn time. Surely you want the satisfaction of putting him in handcuffs?"

There was a time it was all I lived for—seeing Bogachev's face when I revealed I was FBI and he was under arrest. But it's just not important to me now. I'd rather be with Bebe, ensuring her continued safety until that monster is behind bars.

"How are things with Bogachev?" Ken asks. He's been filled in on my current deception—pretending to be in California hunting down Bebe's family.

I grimace slightly. "He's not happy it's taking me so long. Demanding I come back and report face to face on the setback."

Ken's eyes darken with worry. "Has your cover been compromised?"

I shrug. "You never know with Bogachev. He's paranoid by nature, so on one hand, him demanding I fly back across the country to give him a face-to-face report isn't so unusual. But on the other, it could mean he's suspicious of me."

"I think it's safe if we just assume that," Ken suggests. "Your undercover operation is now officially over."

He's not wrong. It would be stupid of us to take anything for granted right now.

Ken and I continue to hash out the game plan until we feel there's no room for any unknowns. It's simple. Bebe and I will park in the designated area, which puts her and the Hijacker within close enough distance to activate the USB device I'd installed. Ken will watch us the entire time, providing armed backup in the slim chance it's needed.

When we're done, we shake hands, and I promise to call him in the morning when I'm ready for the van.

I don't head back to Bebe though.

I have one more thing I need to do.

◆

I PLACE THE keycard against the pad beside the door. When the light turns green, I slowly open the door, trying not to make any noise. I've only been gone about an hour and a half, and I hope Bebe's still sleeping. I want her as fortified as possible for what we have coming tomorrow.

I barely get the door halfway open before I see her on the bed, sitting cross-legged with a cup of hotel brew in her hand. The TV is set to some local news station, and I can hear them reporting about a double murder.

Her eyes come to me, and she gives me a slow but chastising smile. Then her eyes widen as she truly takes me in and her jaw hangs open wide. "What happened to you?" she asks slowly and sounding slightly awed.

I give her a half-assed grin, rubbing my hand over my now-buzzed hair. The stop I had to make after meeting with Ken was to a barbershop. "I figured it was time to cut it all off seeing as how the undercover portion of my job is over. Now it's my disguise."

Bebe just stares in shock a moment before setting her coffee on the bedside table. She uncurls from the bed, then walks to me with a sense of wonderment. I hold still as she approaches, and her eyes roam all over my face.

When she's toe to toe with me, her hands come to my cheeks and she smooths her thumbs over the freshly shaven skin.

"I barely recognize you," she murmurs. "Is this how you normally wear your hair?"

I nod. I was never much for anything other than a short buzz cut all the same length. I had a girlfriend once tell me my cheekbones demanded I not let a hairstyle interfere with my face.

"These cheekbones," Bebe murmurs, grazing her fingertips over them.

I snort with laughter.

"What?" she asks, giggling but not once meeting my eyes. She's still taking in every detail of my face that's been hidden under a beard.

"Not the first time I've heard the cheekbone thing," I admit.

Finally, her gaze meets mine, her expression somberly earnest. "I like it. I really do."

"Not going to miss biker dude Griff?" I tease.

"Well, you still have the tattoos," she points out. "So there's that."

"Yes, the tattoos are definitely mine and staying."

"You were hot before," she says, hands now lacing behind my neck. "In that badass, sinister kind of way.

But now you're just… pretty. Like really, really pretty."

"Nothing emasculating about that," I mutter drily.

She laughs, shaking her head. "No, I just mean… you could be a model or something if this FBI thing doesn't pan out."

I can feel my smooth cheeks heating up from her overt ogling, something that is both weird and pleasing. I mean… I knew Bebe was attracted to me. That much was obvious, but her compliments are so deeply genuine I'm a bit embarrassed.

"You should have woken me up," she chides. "I could have gone with you to meet Ken."

"You should have slept better last night," I counter.

She snorts. "I know damn well you didn't sleep either because I was so busy being restless."

"Your presence wasn't needed," I say, my hands going to her waist. "But are you feeling well rested now?"

"I'm feeling human," she admits.

"Good," I reply, walking her backward to the bed. "Because we have all day to kill, and I'm going to suggest we spend it in bed. Sound good?"

Her smile takes my breath away, and she nods with bright eyes. "Sounds very good."

CHAPTER 23

Bebe

"I N THE MOVIES, I'd be in the back of the van with a really cool equipment setup," I mutter as I work on the laptop propped on my lap.

Griff laughs, his fingers drumming on the steering wheel. "In some scenarios, we do get the fancy van. This isn't one."

No, I suppose it's not needed. Everything I need to do can be done on my laptop. I could have done it in the cafe across the street actually, but we felt being mobile was the better plan in case the signal was weak and we needed to move closer. Ken is situated at said cafe, having texted us to let us know he's at the meal counter at the window and has us in his sights. It doesn't necessarily make me feel better he's there, mainly because I don't think we're in danger.

I don't see how Bogachev could be on to us, and it's not like he's going to stumble across us here. Even if he did—worst-case scenario—come strolling down the block, we're not recognizable. Not only is Griff clean-shaven, but he's wearing a hat and glasses. Same for me, with my long dark hair tucked under a cap.

We're good. I'm sure of it.

It takes me a few minutes to deploy software to help me lock onto the signal from the USB in Bogachev's apartment. While it sends its little feelers out, I twist slightly in the passenger seat to face Griff.

He's watching the bustling streets of Brooklyn, eyes carefully roaming across the landscape.

"Hey," I say softly, and it's all that's needed.

His gaze comes to me, eyebrows slightly raised and mouth curved in welcome of whatever I intend to say. I love that about this man. He's interested—in a profound way—in anything I have to say to him.

"This is it." I reach across, holding my hand out— palm out. He takes it, and we lace fingers. "Not long now, and it's all going to be over with."

"We make a hell of a team," Griff replies.

"Indeed we do." I take him in. Really looking hard at this man who has come to intimately know me both body and soul over the last few weeks, and I've never felt closer to anyone except my son. In my heart, I know Griff is my everything. While this may be the end of a particular saga in our lives, it's not the end of us. "I need to tell you something, and I'm nervous to do it."

"You can tell me anything," he assures me.

I know this. I have absolute trust in him that I can

do exactly that. Even if what I tell him isn't exactly reciprocated, I trust him enough to know he'll get there. I just know it.

"I love you." The words are simple, yet the surety in my voice reverberates between us. "I've never said those words to anyone but my mom and son, but I'm giving them to you to do with what you want. Just know they're not given lightly."

I don't even hold my breath, waiting for his reaction. Whatever it may be, I know I'll be a winner regardless. Griff's eyes lighten, the green going pale but not in a cold way. Instead, his expression warms and goes soft with pleasure.

He opens his mouth, and I know I'm going to get everything I had hoped for in return.

Except a monstrous sound erupts from behind us— an explosion, I think. The van rocks so hard my laptop slides off my lap. Griff's arms go up as he throws himself toward me, and I get a brief, almost slow-motion glimpse of smoke and debris flying past his driver's side window.

His arms come around my shoulders, and he protectively pushes my head down toward the center console.

"What in the fuck?" he growls as he holds me there for several seconds. Then I feel his body go taut, and he rears backward. I open my eyes, seeing him twist toward the driver's window. People are running north up the street, screaming.

Griff sticks his head slightly out the window, looking left toward the café, and my stomach pitches when he snarls, "Goddamn it, motherfucker."

I shift in my seat, peering back through the van to the tinted windows in the double rear doors. The cafe where Ken was sitting is on fire, and there's a large, blackened hole in the sidewalk right in front of it. The glass where he would have been sitting is in shards on the ground, and injured people stagger out the door.

"Was... was... that a bomb?" I ask.

He doesn't respond, merely pulling his head back in the window and putting his hand on the key to crank the engine as his eyes come to mine. "We've got to go. It's Boga—"

When his words fall flat is when I feel the barrel of a gun press against the back of my head through the open passenger window. Griff's eyes flare for a moment before his jaw locks so hard I'm afraid his teeth might crack.

I freeze in place as I hear the door unlatch, knowing whoever is on the other side of that gun is opening the van. My heart is pounding so hard I'm afraid it might explode from my chest, and I'm immediately covered in a cold sweat. Without a doubt, it's the worst fear I've ever experienced in my life as I realize how fragile my mortality is. All I can think about is never seeing Aaron again.

"Move over," a man says in a thick, Russian accent.

"Do as he says," Griff says quickly but with a level of calm in his voice that amazes me.

And strangely, it slightly soothes my fear because I know Griff is smart, capable, and will protect me better than anyone else could.

"Slowly," the Russian adds.

I slide toward the center, not yet even knowing exactly who is coming in the van behind me. All I can do is look to Griff for assurance, but his eyes are locked on the man who has a gun on me.

"You don't have to do this, Karl," Griff warns in a low voice.

Karl? He knows this guy, which means he's Bogachev's man.

It happens quickly. The Russian bands an arm around my waist and pulls me half onto his lap, the gun barrel now going to the corner of my jaw.

"Drive," he orders Griff. "And do it fast or I'll put a bullet in her brain."

There's no hesitation. Griff quickly cranks the van, shifts it into drive, and pulls away from the curb. With the explosion behind us, the traffic in front of us is clear up through the next intersection.

"Turn right," the Russian man orders.

Griff complies, following another series of directions Karl gives with curt efficiency without ever once moving the gun from my jaw. We move several blocks away from the explosion, my stomach hurting over the people who may have been hurt or killed in that explosion.

A clear diversionary tactic that was used so we could be hijacked. And there's no doubt who's behind this.

The question is how exactly had he found out what was going on?

"Where are we going?" Griff asks the man holding the gun.

"Shut up and drive," Karl barks in return.

Griff ignores him. "You don't need to do this. I can help you out of this situation. I can guarantee you immunity if you—"

"Shut the fuck up or I will kill her," the Russian screams, clearly rattled by the situation.

"Okay," Griff says quickly. "Okay... just calm down."

"Turn right up there." The man motions, briefly moving the gun from my face to point to an alley. "Drive all the way to the back, put it in park, and cut the engine."

The alley is about half a block long, and it ends with an elevated loading dock. Not something big enough to accommodate an actual semi with a trailer, but more the size of a delivery van or cargo truck.

Griff pulls in perpendicular to the platform, which has a small staircase leading up to it from the pavement. He puts it in park and turns the engine off.

Karl leans forward so he can look at Griff. "Now, we're going to get out of the van and walk up those stairs to the doors. I'm going to have my gun on her the entire time. Try something funny or try to run, and I'm not going to hesitate in shooting her. Understand?"

Griff's eyes slide to me as he answers. "I won't run. I'm not leaving her."

His message is clear. We're in this together, and he's never going to abandon me.

"Let's go," the man says in his thick accent.

He opens the door, and I'm pulled out of the van. I scrabble a little until I gain my footing, and his free hand bands around my upper arm like a vise grip. The gun goes to my back, pressing into my spine, and we wait for Griff to join us.

Griff comes around the back of the van, hands held out loosely to his side as he walks slowly. Showing Karl he's not a threat, although I can see in his eyes he is.

He's very much a threat, and he's just waiting for the right opportunity to make his move. My gaze goes to the double metal doors leading into the brick building. I have no clue where we are or what type of business this is, but I'm fairly sure what waits inside is dire.

"Move," the Russian orders Griff, jerking his head toward the stairs. Griff moves past us, but he briefly locks eyes with me. Within his expression, I see the words he didn't get a chance to say before the explosion occurred.

The big man pulls me along behind Griff, and we follow him up the stairs. At the top, he orders, "Doors are unlocked. Go in."

Griff merely looks over his shoulder, as if refusing the request. The gun moves from my spine to the back of my head again. It's enough to dissuade Griff from antagonizing the guy any further. He reaches his hand out, places it on the knob on the right-sided door, and twists.

It opens easily, and we're greeted with blackness from inside.

"Go in," the man orders. Griff takes a tentative step inside. I'm pulled along, close on Griff's heels.

Once we're all the way inside, the Russian raises the hand holding the gun. Before I can even cry out in warning, he's bringing it down hard on the back of Griff's head.

The connection of metal to skull is sickening. Bile rises in my throat. I release a pained cry of distress as Griff sinks to his knees. While the blow was vicious, it doesn't render him unconscious. The man lets me go, steps closer to Griff, and hits him again. Tears fill my eyes as Griff goes silent, slumping onto the concrete floor.

My brain screams to run or even attack the man as he glares down at Griff, but I'm frozen in place, terrified one wrong move will result in me getting killed sooner rather than later. I also know in my heart I can't leave Griff helpless like this.

The man turns, gives me a short glance, and then moves toward the door. He flips a switch, and an overhead light comes on. We're in what looks to be an abandoned commercial kitchen, so I'm guessing we're in an old restaurant that's gone out of business.

He kicks the door closed, then motions toward two folding wooden chairs next to a stainless-steel table. On top, there's a coil of thin, white rope.

"Sit down," he orders.

My gaze goes to Griff, who is motionless on the floor. With the overhead light on, I'm able to see blood on the back of his head. Perhaps I should make my stand here. I've always been told to fight, kick, scream, and claw. *Never let yourself get taken or tied up.*

"Sit down," the man says, and my eyes snap to him. He points the gun not at me, but at Griff. "Or else I'll shoot him."

He's using the same tactics to make me obey as he did with Griff. Any hint of a threat, and I don't doubt he'd shoot. He's already taken part in the possible murder of those people in the cafe—possibly Ken Battersham—as well as kidnapping. He's not afraid to use that gun, I'm sure.

I move to one of the wooden chairs and sit. The man moves to the counter, then places the gun there before picking up the rope. "This gun is in easy reach. You so much as breath wrong, I will use it. I've got orders to eliminate you both if you give me any trouble. You should know, whatever I do going forward, I'll sleep easy tonight."

I believe him. He doesn't have an ounce of remorse in the tone of his voice or his expression.

So I sit still and let the man tie me up. My arms are pulled behind the chair and tied at the wrist, then the rope is secured to the outer braces of the chair near my hips.

When he's done, the Russian takes the gun and tucks in into the back waistband of his jeans. He trudges over to Griff, then gives him a hard kick in the back. I grimace, my heart shredding over the abuse, but Griff doesn't make a sound. It makes me relieved he didn't feel that blow.

Seemingly satisfied he's clearly incapacitated, the enormous man squats and hooks his arms under Griff's. With a mighty heave, he lifts him and waddles backward to the chair beside me. He manages to turn and dump Griff's weight there. Sagging to the side, his shoulder bumps up against the counter and his legs splay outward. I can see the blood trickling down the back of his neck, and my fingers actually stretch out toward him in a vain attempt to touch him. To reassure myself he's still warm and at least alive.

I watch silently as the Russian places the gun on the counter again, then proceeds to tie Griff to the chair. He doesn't move at all, but I take comfort in seeing the rise and fall of his chest.

That comfort flees the moment the Russian tightens the last knot and moves away from Griff.

From the corner of the kitchen, deep in the shadows where the light above doesn't reach, movement catches my eye.

A man steps forward, hands clasped placidly in front of his body and his lips curved upward in a leering grin.

Anatoly Bogachev.

My stomach clenches in a tight mixture of fear, disgust, and shame for what he did to me.

All of it.

The servitude, the rape, and the ruination of my life.

Yes, I made bad choices for which I've atoned and paid the price. But this man took everything from me. In this moment, I want nothing more than to be the one to kill him.

CHAPTER 24

Griffin

CONSCIOUSNESS COMES SLOWLY and only because the pain in the back of my head won't let me continue to sleep. It's sharp and pounding... *Boom, boom, boom.*

My eyes flutter open, but there's a bright light, causing the pain to intensify. I immediately shut them again, confused over everything.

Why do I hurt?

Where am I?

What day is it?

Where is Bebe?

Bebe!

My eyes fly open, ignoring the bright light and torment going on inside my head.

"Griff?" I hear her voice from my left, realizing I'm slumped over and leaning up against something cold.

I try to straighten, but my arms won't move.

"Are you okay?" Bebe asks, and she sounds terrified.

It gives me energy and purpose, and I lift my head

enough to turn it toward her voice.

She's right beside me, and my gut tightens when I see the terror in her eyes. My entire body lurches toward her, still not understanding why it can't quite move the way I'm commanding. It goes nowhere, but the pain slicing through my head almost makes me pass out. I struggle to keep my eyes focused on Bebe, grimacing through the hurt and confusion.

Her eyes stay locked on me before moving just slightly past me to my right. I see resignation in her gaze, and it scares me.

Twisting in the opposite direction to take in my surroundings, I get the sense I'm in a commercial kitchen. Memories flood as I remember the explosion, the Russian guy taking us to a building, and then blackness.

And then I spot Anatoly Bogachev casually leaning against a stainless-steel counter just a mere three feet from me. It's the same counter I'm currently slumped against, and Bogachev towers over me.

His smile is triumphant and bitterly cold. "Hello, Griffin Moore."

The pain and the fuzziness in my head abate. It strikes me immediately he said my real name, which means he knows I'm FBI. And since he has effectively kidnapped a federal agent, I realize he has no intention of letting me out of here alive. The same probably goes for

Bebe.

"Go take care of the van," Bogachev says quietly while still staring at me. The order confuses me. Perhaps I'm not as clearheaded as I thought.

But there's movement behind Bogachev, and the Russian comes into view. He gives a curt nod at his boss before quietly exiting the double doors we had entered earlier.

I imagine that van will be driven to the nearest chop shop and disassembled within the hour, no trace of it remaining for the police to find.

Bogachev straightens, pointing toward the door the Russian had just exited. "Good guy. Owe a lot to him for pulling this off."

"Good guy?" Bebe snarls in outrage. "He blew up a cafe. Probably killed innocent people."

Shaking his head, Bogachev gives a faux expression of shock. "Oh, he didn't drop the bomb. Another one of my trusted good guys did that, creating the necessary diversion so you two could be snatched." Moving his attention to me, he adds, "But Karl was the one who confirmed some suspicions I'd had about you."

"How's that?" I ask between gritted teeth, clenched partly from anger and partly from pain.

Bogachev moves to stand right in front of Bebe and me. He's dressed in a designer suit in a light gray, complete with a blue silk tie and a matching kerchief in his pocket. His wavy hair is styled to perfection, his manicured hands clasped at his front.

He gives me a tight smile. "It didn't sit right with me when you came to New York last week to tell me you'd killed Bebe. I mean, I bought it at first. I thought you taking her out with a fake overdose was brilliant. I was quite proud of you actually. But you should have left it at that. If so, I probably would have been none the wiser."

"Left it at that?" Bebe asks.

Bogachev doesn't even spare her a glance. His attention stays focused on me. "In the three years you worked for me, you'd never showed that kind of initiative. I mean, you did your job and did it well, but you always flew under the radar. Did anything I asked of you, but nothing more or less. You did the things I hired you to do. You had my back. You protected me. But you never gave me more. Now, of course, I realize you were just trying to get in deep, get me comfortable with you while waiting for the right time to strike. So when you told me about Bebe's kid and how you should go after him, it struck me as... odd."

I hold back a groan of frustration. Just that one little move—to gain more time away from Bogachev so I could work with Jameson to bring him down—was ultimately the downfall in my cover. It was a stupid mistake, and I should have known better.

"It didn't make sense to me," Bogachev continues.

He seems to have a need to make sure I understand just how smart he is, and I'm okay with that. The longer he talks, the longer Bebe and I stay alive until I can figure out how to get us out of this mess. "I was suspicious, but I really couldn't put my finger on anything. But then Karl told me that you'd stayed in my house after our meeting. He said you'd told him you were using the bathroom and well… some people wouldn't think that was odd. People use the bathroom all the time."

I can tell he's enjoying this. The story of how smart he is and how he can't ever be taken for granted. This is all true, of course, but I don't regret anything. We made the decision to go in and have me attempt to plant that USB knowing we could be caught. It was a risk that was approved all the way up the FBI chain of command.

But I am getting a bit tired of hearing his pompous retelling, so I make him skip forward. "Blah, blah, blah," I taunt. "So you got suspicious. I'm guessing you decided to look at the camera feeds and saw me go into your room?"

Bogachev flushes red with anger, his eyes narrowing. "Manners, Griff, or I might have to put an end to this sooner rather than later."

These words are not shocking, because I know how he wants this to end. But Bebe makes a distressed sound. She's terrified, and I hate I can't take the time to comfort her. It's good I've got Bogachev focused on me as I try to figure a way out of this.

"So you saw me plant the USB in your room?" I say, wanting to engage him in conversation.

Buying time.

There was a GPS on the van. It's standard procedure to have one. Perhaps it will lead to our rescue.

Except I know that's unlikely. The bomb was a brilliant diversionary tactic. There would be so much chaos caused from that it would have taken way too long for anyone to know we were missing, particularly with our liaison, Ken, potentially hurt or killed in the blast. My gut swirls with emotion over the thought.

"Admittedly," Bogachev says in response to my question. "I was a bit shocked over your actions. Planting something in my room. You can imagine the betrayal I felt, realizing you weren't who you said you were. What was the device supposed to do anyway?"

"You mean you didn't remove it?" I ask, giving a slight tug against my bonds. Without looking down, I can tell it's rope. I'm secured to what seems to be a wooden dining chair.

Not a flimsy chair, either. Seems very solid.

"Of course I removed it from my TV," Bogachev scoffs as if I asked the dumbest question in the world. "Had some of my best people look at it, and we couldn't quite figure it out. I mean… I suspected it was to steal data from me, so I immediately moved my computers and servers off-site. Plugged that little USB back into the TV, and I waited for you to make your move. Knew it wouldn't be long."

Christ, this is bad. My cover blown, caught by an egomaniac, and worst yet, I dragged Bebe into it with me.

"But how did you find us? How did you even know we were here in New York?" Bebe asked, and I'm pleased her voice sounds strong. I briefly move my attention from Bogachev to her. And yes, she's scared, but she's not cowed.

Bogachev shifts toward Bebe. "With my resources, you should have figured I have all the right people on my payroll."

"Ken?" she gasps in shock.

"No," I say confidently, and Bogachev swings back my way. "Ken was clean. No way you breached the FBI. I'm guessing local police. They are on liaison with us today. Provided the city van and were alerted to give us a wide berth and not to interfere with our work."

I get a smug grin in return. "You're smarter than I gave you credit for. But not smart enough to suspect I was on to you."

"I knew it was a risk," I grit out, getting tired of him wanting to rub my face in it. I pull my legs in slightly, planting my boots solidly on the tile floor. If I'm going to make a move, it's going to be soon. I'm feeling slightly stronger now I've had some time to get my bearings. My head still hurts like a motherfucker, but I've got the desperation to protect Bebe fueling me.

Apparently, Bogachev is as done with me as I am with him because he moves a foot over, putting himself right in front of Bebe's chair. It's a clear statement he's done talking to me.

Giving her a broad smile, almost prideful in nature, he almost purrs, "And look at you, Bebe. You know, you were my brightest star. I had such high hopes for you."

"Go fuck yourself," she growls. Even though I don't want her to antagonize him into doing something, I'm proud of her backbone.

His smile turns feral and malicious. He bends at the waist, putting his face closer to hers. I pull against the ropes, testing to see if there's any give.

I give Bebe credit. She doesn't shrink away from him. Instead, she glares with hard, unforgiving eyes.

His hand comes up, and he almost tenderly glides his knuckles across her cheek. Anger sweeps through me so hot I actually feel chilled from it. That he would dare touch her in such an intimate way makes me itch to beat him to a slimy pulp.

"I'll never forget how sweet you were," Bogachev murmurs to Bebe in a low rumble of appreciation.

For a moment, I don't understand what that means. Bebe's expression slackens, her eyes dulling a bit.

"I'll never forget how much you wanted it," he whispers, but the words are harsh and grating on my ears. I can feel my blood pressure rising as understanding starts to dawn on me. I mean... I think I know what he's saying, but I don't want to believe it.

"I never wanted it," Bebe hisses. "You merely wanted to control me. Scare me."

I lurch against my bonds, trying to reach Bogachev, but I'm held tight. My pulse is pounding so hard my ears feel muffled, and I'm slightly dizzy.

"Want me to prove you wrong?" Bogachev taunts, moving even closer to her.

"What is he talking about?" I demand in a barking sort of shout. But I know what he means. I fucking know... and I'm going to kill the bastard.

Bogachev doesn't pay me any attention, merely tilting his head to level a soft, proprietary smile at Bebe. But it's me he addresses. "Oh, Bebe and I are very intimate with each other."

My blood turns to ice, my body freezing in place.

Bebe turns away from him, but she won't look at me. She grits her teeth in disgust, and I can see the shame on her face.

It does something to me.

Changes me forever.

That he would make her feel that way enrages me.

"You wanted it, Bebe," Bogachev murmurs in a

smarmy, overly sexual way. "You know you did."

She whips her head back, teeth bared and snarling. "I never wanted it. You're a disgusting pig. The only way you can get it is to pay for it or take it by force. You're a sad little man with a tiny, pathetic dick and—"

I roar with rage, having heard enough. When I push to my feet, I'm immediately hampered by the chair that comes with me off the floor. I'm huddled over, forced into a bent position by the chair, but my legs are free.

Fucking bad move, Karl. Not tying my legs.

I lurch toward Bogachev, who is still crouched in front of Bebe. I have just a moment where his head is able to turn my way, eyes flared wide with surprise at my sudden move, and then I'm crashing my entire body into him. I drive him back several feet, pumping my legs hard. Vaguely, I hear Bebe scream. As we near the wall, I shift my body slightly so the chair takes most of the impact. There's an explosion of wood, and my shoulders feel like they're nearly wrenched from the sockets.

Bogachev grunts with pain as we fall to the floor, him taking most of my weight as I crash on top of him. For a split second, we're torso to torso, me on top, and I don't waste the opportunity. I rear my head back and slam it forward, aiming my forehead for the bridge of his nose.

Unfortunately, I catch too much of his forehead and not enough of his nose. The impact concusses me, making my vision go blurry. The only consolation is the curse of pain from Bogachev and knowing he's hurt as bad as I am.

But he's got two advantages over me—he's not hampered by rope or pieces of wooden chair and he didn't take two strikes from a gun to the back of his head earlier.

With a mighty heave, he pushes me off his body. I come to rest on my side. He scrambles to his feet, and I recognize the urgency for me to do the same. I'm relieved to find the seat, back of the chair, and legs have all come apart at the joints, but pieces of wood are still tied to my wrists and arms, effectively binding my upper body.

I manage to lunge to my feet, ignoring the pain all over my body and the dizziness the move causes.

Bogachev is quicker than I am. Because his arms are free, he has no problem reaching inside his suit jacket and pulling out a gun.

He levels it at me, his chest heaving hard and a trickle of blood running from a cut in his forehead down the side of his nose. Peeling his lips back in a grimace, he glares hatred at me.

I have a choice. *Keep fighting or surrender.*

Not really a choice at all.

I spring toward him, hoping to catch him somewhat off guard. His eyes flare in shock, not expecting me to charge. Bebe screams again.

I lower my shoulder, intent on barreling into him

once more, but the sound of the gun going off causes me to stumble.

No wait… something hitting me in my chest causes me to stumble.

Down to one knee I go, immediately becoming weak as a baby, but not feeling a damn thing otherwise.

"No," Bebe shrieks, and it's only then I realize I've been shot.

CHAPTER 25

Bebe

"**G**RIFF," I SCREAM when the gun goes off. I see a bloom of dark wetness spreading across his black t-shirt, just under his collarbone, but he's not thrown backward by the force of the bullet. In fact, he takes one more step before his leg wobbles and he goes down to one knee.

He hunches over, head hanging low, and I think he might just topple over. My heart slams painfully in my chest, and I have to blink my eyes hard to dispel the welling tears.

Bogachev remains still, his arm extended with the gun pointed at Griff.

Slowly, Griff raises his head. Even though his eyes are glazed with pain, his expression is one of determination. A lump forms in my throat as he pushes himself up... miraculously rising with just the power of his legs as his arms are still entwined with rope and wooden pieces of chair. He's bleeding badly and wobbling, but his chin is lifted stubbornly as if daring Bogachev to finish him off.

"Anatoly," I cry out, hoping to take the heat away from Griff.

Bogachev is no fool though. He keeps his gaze locked on Griff—who is still very much a threat—but his head tilts slightly my way to indicate he's listening. The gun drops slightly.

"Please don't do this," I beg him. "Just leave Griff alone and take me. Do whatever you want to me, just…" My voice cracks, emotion clogging my throat. I can't bear it if Griff dies. I don't care what happens to me—I just need to save him.

"She's begging me," Bogachev says smugly, and a low growl emits from Griff. "It's a beautiful sound, isn't it?"

"Fuck you," Griff snarls. "Fuck you straight to hell."

I'm not prepared for his sudden move, but neither is Bogachev. Griff lunges at him, and he's momentarily stunned into inaction. Another scream tears free from my throat, but it's drowned out by the sound of the double doors bursting open. Sunlight temporarily blinds me. I hear gunshots—three to be exact—and I see Griff slamming into Bogachev where they both crash to the floor.

I turn fearfully to the door, expecting to see Karl there with a smoking gun. Instead, I'm stunned to see Kynan with a grim expression and a gun leveled at the mass of legs and limbs on the floor. Behind him, Cruce and Saint move into the room, sweeping their guns and gazes left and right to ensure there's no hidden threats.

"Griff," I cry helplessly. I whip my head toward Kynan. "Help him, please."

Cruce moves to me, holstering his gun, then his hands go to the knots at my wrists. My gaze goes back to Griff, and a flare of hope pulses within me when he rolls off Bogachev with a loud groan. I scan his body, but I can't see anything other than the dark blood spreading even further over his chest.

Kynan moves carefully toward them, his gun leveled at Bogachev, who lays utterly still on the floor. I can't keep my eyes off Griff, though, who is now on his back and staring at the ceiling while seeming to gasp for breath.

Cruce removes the last piece of rope from me, releasing me from the chair, and I try to spring up to get to Griff. Cruce's hands come to my shoulder, holding me in place. "Just wait a minute."

I struggle against him, and he orders again, "Just give Kynan a moment."

Kynan?

My gaze goes back to him as he inches carefully toward Bogachev, gun still aimed at him. I take a breath, focusing on the supine man. His eyes are closed, and I can't see if his chest is rising and falling. I can see a bright red bloom of blood in the center of his chest, and it's the first time I understand... at least one of those gunshots I

SAWYER BENNETT

heard had been reserved for Bogachev.

Kynan squats, puts his fingers to Bogachev's neck, and holds still for a long moment. His gaze comes to me, and he gives a slight shake of his head.

That asshole is dead, and I can't find it within myself to care.

Cruce's hands go slack on my shoulders, and I bolt from the chair. I fall to my knees at his side, hands on his cheeks as I bend over him. "Griff... please, please, please don't die."

His eyes are dulled slightly, but he manages a smiling sort of grimace. "You can't get rid of me that easily."

"Ambulance is on the way," I hear Saint say from near the door, but I don't take my eyes off Griff.

Kynan moves in beside me, pulling Griff's shirt up so he can survey the damage. There's a single bullet hole just below his collarbone, mercifully high above where his heart lays.

"Are you hit anywhere else?" I ask, distinctly remembering I'd heard three gunshots.

Griff shakes his head and then coughs, a slightly gurgling sound that alarms me. "I'm pretty sure you'll find three bullet holes in Bogachev."

I'm immediately relieved he has that presence of mind. That he counted the same gunshots I did—and knowing Bogachev is dead on the floor beside him and he only has one wound—and that the others hit their

262

mark.

Griff's gaze moves from me to Kynan. "Thanks, man."

Kynan doesn't respond. Instead, he casts a worried glance over at Cruce.

"What?" I ask Kynan, my fear already compounded by what just went down and the fact the man I love has a bullet in his chest.

Kynan doesn't respond. He takes my hands from Griff's face, then places them over the bullet hole in his chest that's leaking blood. "Keep pressure on him. Ambulance will be here soon."

Without looking, Kynan pushes to his feet and moves over to where Cruce and Saint wait by the door. I gaze at Griff, who seems to understand the current of unspoken emotion swirling around everyone.

"What's going on?" I whisper.

"Kynan just killed a man," he replies, his voice surprisingly strong given his injury.

"Good," I reply shrilly. "Because he was getting ready to kill you."

Griff's smile is wan. His hand comes up to cover mine where it's pressed onto his wound. "He has no authority here. No jurisdiction. He's a civilian—"

I lean in closer, putting my face near his. "I don't care. Bogachev was getting ready to kill you. Kynan was defending you and protecting me. Surely they'll see—"

"Ambulance is here," Saint says, cutting over me. The sound of the siren gets closer and closer.

I give a confident smile to Griff. "No more talking. Let's just get you taken care of. We'll worry about Kynan later, okay?"

He coughs again, grimaces, and nods.

There's a flurry of activity. Paramedics come in first with a gurney and bags of gear. They dress the wound and start an IV while one of the paramedics gets on the phone with an emergency room doctor to apprise them of the situation. He tells me they'll take him straight into surgery.

As they're loading Griff into the ambulance, I see Kynan, Cruce, and Saint each talking to three separate police officers. Their expressions are grim, and I have a moment of fear shoot through me.

Is Kynan going to be in trouble over this?

I told Griff I didn't care that he shot and killed Bogachev, but now that Griff is on his way to get medical help, I know I really didn't mean to be dismissive of Kynan's plight.

Spinning from the gurney, I trot over to Kynan and the cop he's talking to. "I'm sorry to interrupt, but can I speak to Kynan for a moment?"

I don't give the police officer time to argue with me, simply pull Kynan away by the arm. We step several feet to the side before I ask, "How much trouble are you in?"

His smile is confident and reassuring. I don't trust it a bit. "Don't worry about me. Just head to the hospital to be with Griff, and we'll meet you there when we finish up. I'm sure a police officer will come there to get your statement too."

"Will you really?" I ask, feeling like I'm going to hurl. "Or are you going to be arrested?"

"I'm not going to get arrested," he promises me.

I don't believe him. "Promise on Joslyn's life."

Kynan's face clouds over. "That I'll never do. But you don't need to worry, Bebe."

"Ma'am," one of the paramedics calls. When I look over to him, I see Griff has been loaded into the ambulance. "We need to go."

"Get going," Kynan says, his hand coming to my shoulder and squeezing.

I hesitate just a moment, but then nod. "Okay. See you at the hospital."

◆

THE GLASS DOOR to Griff's hospital room slides open with a soft hiss, and Kynan walks in. I immediately rise from the reclining chair a nurse had brought in a few hours ago.

"How's he doing?" Kynan murmurs, nodding toward Griff.

I move over to him, leaning in to speak softly so as

not to wake Griff. "Good. Surgery was pretty easy. The bullet went through and didn't damage much of anything. They said he'll probably be released tomorrow. He's been sleeping the anesthesia off."

"Good," Kynan replies with relief. "That's really good."

"What about you?" I whisper urgently. "An FBI agent came and talked to me while Griff was in surgery, but he wouldn't tell me anything."

Well, that's not exactly true. He told me Ken Battersham was severely injured in the bombing Bogachev set into motion. He's in critical condition in the ICU, and Griff is going to be devastated when I finally tell him.

"It's all good," Kynan says, and I dare to hope.

"I need more than that," I demand.

"They aren't going to press any charges against me," he says, and my knees go weak with relief. I put a hand on the wall for support. "The FBI intervened with the prosecuting attorney's office, and they also put some pressure on the police because someone inside the precinct leaked the information to Bogachev in the first place. But bottom line… I was acting in defense of you and Griff. They get it."

Letting out a sigh that completely deflates my lungs, I feel my eyes fill with unwanted tears. I try to blink them away, but they keep coming, spilling over the edge and streaming down my cheeks as I realize it's all over.

I try to hold it in, which is a bad idea because I end up releasing a horrible, racking sob that has my head whipping toward Griff to see if it woke him. He slumbers on, but I'm immediately pulled into Kynan's arms.

The minute I'm wrapped in his secure, strong embrace, I let loose. Burying my face into his chest, I let the tears flow and I don't hold back in the slightest.

"Shh." His hand rubs the middle of my back. "It's all over, Bebe."

I cry even harder, muffling my sobs into his strong chest.

"Shh, shh, shh," he urges, hands going to the side of my head to push me back from his chest a bit so he can look down at me. He's blurry from the cascade of tears flowing, but I blink them back. "Hey... it's over, Bebe."

I nod furiously, blinking away more tears. "It's over."

"Then why the tears?" he asks gently.

Why indeed?

It's monumental, really. "Because I'm finally free. Free of my past and the terror Bogachev always held over me. Free of my mistakes and the losses they produced. I'm just free... and it's overwhelming."

Smiling, Kynan nods in understanding. He glances at Griff. "That guy there is part of your newfound freedom."

I look over my shoulder at the hospital bed where my

man sleeps peacefully, thanks to the pain medications. My lips curve upward, even as a few more tears slip free.

Yeah, I'm finally free… and Griff is part of the future now spread wide before me.

CHAPTER 26

Griffin

"**A**RE YOU ABOUT ready to go?" Bebe asks as she zips the large suitcase we'd brought with us to New York a mere four days ago. "I'm going to check the bathroom one more time."

She's been in mother mode since I was released from the hospital yesterday. I'd been in just a little over twenty-four hours, but it was so late in the day by the time I finally got released we decided to stay the night in a hotel before driving back to Pittsburgh today.

Yesterday afternoon and evening, I spent most of the time in bed sleeping. Granted, my gunshot wound wasn't overly serious—infection being the thing they were most worried about and why they wanted to get IV antibiotics in me. But there was a level of exhaustion I didn't feel like battling, so I was grateful for the extra day of rest before we traveled.

Bebe was by my side the entire time, hovering over me any time I woke from a nap, wanting to do something for me. I assured her I was fine, let her feed me when she was hungry, and I slept hard.

But this morning, I'm ready to get on with things. I'm going to be on leave from the FBI for at least a week while I recuperate, and there's no place I'd rather be than back in Pittsburgh with Bebe. Not to mention, I don't technically have a home right now. I'd given up my D.C. apartment years ago when I went undercover, but that's irrelevant.

The point being... I don't want to leave Bebe's side right now. While I got shot, she's been through more of an emotional turmoil than anyone else, and I'm a bit worried about her.

Okay, a lot worried about her. I learned things about her that I never imagined, and I need some closure with it. I need to know if she's okay now that Bogachev's dead.

She crosses the room, briefly disappears into the bathroom, then reappears carrying the small shampoo and conditioner bottles the hotel provides. She holds them up with a sheepish smile. "I can never leave these behind."

From my position sitting on the edge of the bed, I watch as she moves back to the suitcase and stuffs the mini bottles into a side pocket. Turning back to me, she says, "Okay... I'll call the valet to bring our car to the front. I can handle the suitcase so we won't need a bellman."

"Hey," I say softly, holding my hand out. "Come here a minute and let's talk."

Bebe tilts her head, her expression quizzical. "Are you okay?"

I level a chastising look, patting the mattress beside me. "Get your butt over here and sit."

There's no hesitation. She takes a seat beside me, angling her body slightly so she can look me in the eye. "What's up? You're not having second thoughts about going to Pittsburgh, are you?"

"No, not at all," I assure her, taking her hand in mine. "It's just… we haven't had a chance to talk about what happened. And I'm worried about you."

Bebe blinks in surprise, leaning in slightly. "Worried about me? You're the one who was shot… almost killed. Why would you be worried about me?"

My heart is heavy that I need to press this upon her, but I need to know. "He raped you."

She doesn't flinch. Blink. Doesn't even suck in a deep breath.

Instead, Bebe smiles. A soft one… a little nostalgic, but I detect nothing else there. No sadness, bitterness, or shame.

"He did," she replies simply. "It was before I stole the codes. I'd wanted out, and it was his way of putting me in my place. He also threatened Aaron's life. It was effective because I went through with it."

"He raped you," I repeat, this time not to get verification but to let her know how that affected me. "And I was so angry when I learned that. Rageful. In my entire life, I've never wanted to kill someone. But I wanted him dead. I tried to kill him, Bebe. Had my hands been free... he'd be dead because of me instead of Kynan. That's how furious I was—I was willing to take a man's life because of it. And now... all I can think is if I felt that way about it—had such strong emotions because it happened to my girlfriend—what in the hell were you possibly going through? You're the one who was violated and destroyed by that man. What the hell were you feeling? How did you survive that? What are you feeling now? Before we get in the car and head off to a future together, I need to know how you're doing and what I can do to make it better. How do I fix things for you that might still be broken? Just tell me—"

"Stop." Bebe's voice is gentle but commanding, causing my mouth to snap shut. Though not needed, she even places her fingertips against my mouth while giving me an empathetic look. "I'm sorry you had to hear about it that way. Bogachev didn't bring that up for my benefit, but to taunt you. He was making you suffer. It was a punishment for you, and I'm sorry you had to go through that."

My hand locks around her wrist, and I pull her fingers off my lips. I can't hide the small quiver of anger in my tone. "You're sorry? Why the fuck are you apologizing for that douchebag?"

"I'm apologizing for myself," she clarifies. "I should have told you. I shouldn't have let you find out that way, and I should have told you because I care for you deeply. I trust you with my life, so I should have trusted that secret with you as well. The only reason I didn't was because it honestly didn't seem important in the grand scheme of things. I'd dealt with it, Griff. It was behind me."

"Truly?" It doesn't quite seem plausible to me, but, then again, Bebe Grimshaw is without a doubt the strongest, most resilient woman I've ever known.

"Yes, truly," she assures me. "I mean… I struggled with it for a long, long time. Went through a phase where I thought I'd deserved it—you know, as a punishment for my crimes. But I dealt with it. I talked to a lot of other women in prison who were victims of sexual crimes. I learned how to heal and forgive myself. Granted, Bogachev coming back into my life sort of dredged things up again, but God help me, Griff… I'm glad he's dead. I don't want to be that type of person, but I'm happy he's dead rather than facing justice in the courts. Because right now, knowing he can't hurt another person or terrorize another woman, I've never been more peaceful with my past than I am right now."

And it's peace that suffuses me as I take in her confident expression and the earnest gleam in her eyes. She's truly okay, and I'm totally all right with the fact Bogachev's death is part of the reason.

I know I'm glad he's dead. Glad Kynan burst through those doors and popped him with a few bullets.

Speaking of which… a thought strikes me. "Hey, how in the hell did Kynan know where we were?"

Bebe's eyes actually sparkle with mischief, and she laughs. "Well, you know he was worried about me coming to New York and he wasn't pleased the FBI wouldn't let Jameson be involved in the actual takedown, so he took it upon himself to stalk us."

I frown. "Come again?"

"They were parked down the next block from us, watching our van," she says, and my jaw drops in astonishment. "Of course, the explosion was between us and them, so there was no way they could just follow our van once Karl kidnapped us. But Kynan's always thinking a few steps ahead."

Then Bebe taps her fingertip against one of her earrings. Can't say as I paid them much attention before. They're silver Celtic knots about the size of a dime with a black stone in the center.

"Pretty earrings," I mutter.

"Thanks," she says, beaming back. "Kynan gave them to me as a present the morning we left. He said they were an apology gift for the fight we'd gotten into when I wanted to come to New York and he wouldn't let me."

"Okay," I drawl, clearly not understanding a damn thing.

She taps the earring again. "The stone is a GPS locator."

My eyes flare with respect. "No shit?"

"No shit," she replies with a laugh. "I should have known, too, because I created similar earrings for Joslyn when Jameson was protecting her from a stalker. She was wearing my earrings when she was taken, and it's how we located her. And I never even considered Kynan was doing the same to me. He must have had Dozer whip them up the night before we left."

"So they were able to track us," I murmur in amazement.

"Well, not very easily," she replies with a shake of her head. "It was chaos from the bomb going off. By the time they'd navigated around a few blocks, Karl had a good head start. They had to do a lot of guessing and driving in the general direction we went before they picked up the signal. Luckily, Dozer was able to boost the reception and pick up our trail. They were outside practically the entire time though, listening in with sound amplifiers and recording for evidence. It was when Bogachev brought up the rape that they started to mobilize. They figured things were going to go south at that point. Kynan said he knew you'd never take that sitting down."

"It all worked out kind of perfectly." Fuck if there wasn't a lot of luck involved in the outcome, which makes me even more grateful this woman is alive and well and sitting next to me.

"So, I'm really okay," she reiterates to put my mind fully at ease.

But I'm not.

Fully at ease, I mean. Because, surely, there has to be one more thing that doesn't have resolution. I'm sure it's still bothering her.

"You're okay?" I ask.

She nods brightly. "Promise."

"Nothing else bothering you?" I prompt.

She shakes her head, smile locked in place.

"You're positive?"

"Yup," she chirps.

"Little liar," I chastise in a low voice, putting my right hand to the back of her neck. My left arm is held in place by a sling, not because there was any damage to my actual shoulder joint on the left side by the bullet, but just because movement on that side would hurt like hell. What I hate about this is I'd much rather have gathered her in my arms and pulled her onto my lap, but I have to work within my limitations.

"Liar?" she repeats a little indignantly.

"Oh, come on, Bebe," I drawl in a faux accusatory

way. "Just before the bomb went off, you told me something important. You told me you loved me—that I was your soulmate, and you couldn't live without me. Big stuff you laid at my doorstep."

Her eyebrows draw in, and she glares. "First, I didn't say all that crap about soulmates and not being able to live without you."

I grin. "But you did say you loved me and before I could even reply, everything went *boom*."

"I didn't expect the words back," she mutters. "I don't need them back, so that's not bothering me if you think it is."

"Well, it's bothering me, damn it," I assure with a squeeze to her neck. "I'd intended to tell you right then I'd felt the same. And while one could assume I love you since I'm returning to Pittsburgh with you for the near future, I can't help but be motivated to say the words so you have no doubt."

Bebe stares, eyes wide and yearning. It may not bother her I haven't said it yet, but I can tell she wants it. Her body leans in ever so slightly, as if she's afraid she might miss something she's waited her whole life to hear, and that warms me clear through to my bones.

"I love you, Bebe." Her blue eyes are locked tight onto mine, and I can tell she's memorizing every detail of this moment. I pull her in a bit closer. "I can't say it's a shocking revelation to myself about just how much I love you, because deep down inside, I feel I was always meant to. It feels like you're the open door with a warm light on, just waiting for me after a long journey. And believe me, I have no hesitation walking on through it to be with you."

"Griff," she whispers as her eyes slowly close. A small smile plays at her lips, and I let her savor the moment.

When her eyelids lift and those crystalline blues are locked on me, she says, "I don't know what I did to deserve you. But I'm going to spend every day of my life making sure I don't take the gift that's been handed to me for granted."

It pleases me to hear she feels the same way about me that I do about her. Truly, she's the most amazing gift I ever could have been handed.

I don't have to lean in far to brush my lips against hers. Her sigh is barely audible, but I can feel the joy within it. Pulling back ever so slightly, she whispers against my mouth, "I'm ready to go home."

"Let's do it then."

CHAPTER 27

Bebe

M Y MOM CHECKS the garlic bread in the double oven, which smells heavenly. I've got bubbling lasagna going in the bottom one—a dish I've found I'm quite good at making since I got out of prison. I'm putting the final touches on a salad, cutting up some radishes to layer over the top.

"I think it's ready to come out," my mom murmurs. She and I have spent a lot of time in the kitchen over the last few days since her return from California with my son. We've been cooking and baking or just sipping coffee and chatting. Sometimes, Griff joins us. More often than not, he occupies himself elsewhere while he recuperates, which is code for relaxing in the recliner while watching *Sports Center*. Or like today, he disappeared for a few hours with Aaron to go toss the football. This only after I worried like a henpecking woman over his injury, but he assured me he was fine.

Currently, Griff is with Aaron in the living room. Last time I'd poked my head in there, they were side by side on the couch playing some video game that had them racing cars against each other. They were talking trash and laughing, and it warmed my heart greatly.

"Griff is so good with Aaron," my mom says out of the blue, as if she'd just taken a little trip through my internal thoughts. I startle and send her an incredulous look, but she ignores me, having pulled the garlic bread out of the oven. "Aaron's getting really attached to him."

"So am I," I murmur, my lips quirking up.

She pulls out a serrated bread knife. Using a tea towel to hold over the hot bread, she starts to cut slices. "What's he going to do, do you think?" she asks.

I pick up the sliced radishes, then distribute them over the top of the salad. Nabbing a few paper towels from the dowel in front of me, I wipe my hands dry. "I don't know. He has to report back to D.C. next week."

My mom turns my way. "Will he be medically cleared by then?"

I shrug. "I suppose."

If the way he performed in my bed last night is any indication, he's fit for duty. Sure, he still has a stitched-up wound under his collarbone, but he more than made up for that slight limitation in other ways. I had to bury my face in a pillow to keep from screaming out and alerting my mom and son that Griff is most definitely on the mend.

"Well, it will be nice to figure out what your new

normal is going to be," she says.

Yes, it would. I'll be starting back to work tomorrow, which is a good thing. While it's been nice hanging with my mom and Griff for a few days and spending the extra time with Aaron when he's home from school, I do miss my crew at Jameson and the work we do.

Now if we can just figure out exactly what our future holds, Griff and I would be able to settle into that new normal my mom mentioned.

It's not that we haven't talked about our future to-gether... because we have.

A lot, actually.

First, we've affirmed how much we love each other and are meant for each other. Those words come frequently and with such ease it really does feel a bit like we've settled into our destiny. In fact, we've got a trip planned early next month to travel to New York, so Aaron and I can meet Griff's parents.

We've also talked about career dreams and aspira-tions. Griff asked me point blank if I'd ever leave Jameson—given how his job is based out of Washington, D.C.—and I had to be honest with him. It was as shocking to me as I'm sure it was to him when I told him I would leave Jameson if it was the only way we could be together.

Of course, Griff has come to know me well. He realizes how much I love my work with Kynan and his crew, so while it would have been very easy for Griff to take that admission from me and haul me off to D.C., he instead kept poking at other possibilities.

He asked if I could continue with Jameson from another location. I can, of course. I could also do a commute back and forth if necessary.

On the flip side, we spent a lot of time talking about Griff's love of the FBI. It's what he's wanted to do since he was a little boy, but he wasn't sure if he wanted to stay in cybercrime. He'd transitioned there from white collar, but he also had an interest in counterterrorism. While he technically didn't get to bring Bogachev through the system to a conviction, he'll go down as the one who stopped his reign of crime.

And just last night, Kynan straight out asked me via text if I thought Griff would be interested in coming to work for Jameson. I brought up the idea to him as we lay in bed together, and he wasn't crazy about the idea. Not because he disliked anyone here. On the contrary, he has mad respect for everyone—particularly Kynan, who saved us—but merely because he loves being an FBI agent. Again, he's fulfilling a childhood dream.

So yeah…plenty of talking, but no real idea what we're going to do as a couple for our future.

There's no rush, and we'll get there eventually. It's enough to know we're committed to a life together going forward.

Right now, we'll be happy just reveling in being normal for a change with this nastiness firmly behind us.

Of course, Bogachev's death made national news—not because his cybercrimes were all that interesting to the public, but because he set off a bomb in New York to try to foil an FBI raid. At least that's how it was reported to the media outlets.

The power and pull Kynan continues to exhibit amuses me. There was absolutely no mention of him, me, or Jameson being involved. It was reported Bogachev was killed by an FBI agent during a hostage rescue. There were no mention of leaks from the local police or of poor Ken Battersham, who has an incredibly long recovery ahead of him. The story presented was nowhere near the truth of what actually happened, but that's how we prefer it. It's even possible Kynan called in a token favor from as high up as the president of the United States, because his authority goes that high up in the ranks.

"Well, I hope you two make a decision soon," my mom says, jarring me from my thoughts.

She sounds worried, and I frown. "Why's that?"

Tilting her head, she smirks. "Because I want you to hurry up and secure your happily ever after. As your mother, it's the last thing I have to fret over."

Chuckling, I shake my head and open one of the drawers to search for salad tongs. "Don't worry, Mom.

Griff and I will be fine no matter what."

Finding the tongs, I shove them into the salad and turn toward the hallway separating the kitchen and living room. "Aaron, Griff… dinner's ready."

"Awww… Mom… just ten more minutes," Aaron calls back in a whiny voice only a ten-year-old can carry off with a modicum of cuteness.

"Yeah, Mom," Griff echoes in an exaggerated, petulant voice. "Ten more minutes."

"Now," I say, using my mom voice that may have been quite rusty for the last several years, but still packs a sufficient wallop with the promise of retribution if I'm not obeyed.

"Oh, boy," I hear Griff murmur as the TV goes silent. "Is that her mad voice?"

"Nah," Aaron replies with a snicker. "Not anywhere close to it."

"Then I have no desire to hear her true mad voice," Griff replies.

My mom and I cut looks at each other, grinning.

Griff and Aaron appear in the kitchen, my son moving right to the breakfast nook we've been eating at over the last few nights, which is more intimate than the formal dining room. Griff heads right for me. With no concern that my mom or son may be watching, he wraps his untethered arm around my waist.

He leans down, nuzzles my neck, and murmurs,

"Smells good."

If the women in prison could see me now, they'd think I'd gone crazy as the Bebe Grimshaw they knew wasn't a giggler.

But fuck if I don't do just that, burrowing into Griff's body for a second. My gaze goes to my mom, who pretends she's not reveling in this with that little secret smile as she moves to the oven to grab the lasagna. I glance over to Aaron, who's watching Griff and me with an affable curiosity. It's still a bit odd having a male figure around, and having said male figure pay attention to his mom.

But Aaron knows enough about societal norms to know this direction is a good one. Having a positive male influence in his life is something that's more than beneficial.

Plus, I know my kid.

He's happy if his mom is happy.

I shrug Griff off, playfully pushing him toward the table. My mom and I work in tandem to set everything out. Lasagna, salad, dressings, and drinks. We sit together as a family, and I dish out steamy, gooey piles of Italian goodness onto plates.

We laugh and joke.

We talk about our days.

Aaron and Griff go off on a football tangent, and life is incredibly good.

"So, listen," Griff says after setting his utensils down and wiping his mouth with his napkin. "I had a long talk with my boss today."

This has me sitting straight in my chair, because the tone of his voice is somber. My mom frowns, and Aaron just tilts his head as he continues to chew his food.

"I've been offered a job transfer," he says, and my stomach twists. This is it. I told Griff I'd go with him, wherever he was. He was more important than any job, but it's still going to crush me to leave my friends here. "And, well… it's a big transition for everyone at this table. I don't want to presume anything, so I thought it would be good if we talked it out together. Like a family."

My skin flushes at his casual mention that we're a family, then I'm warmed clear through when Aaron grins in response to that new label.

I can't let silly sentiment hold me back. My desire is to be with Griff no matter what so I assure him, "We'll go wherever the FBI wants to send you. Because we *are* a family now."

"Long as there's football," Aaron adds. "I'm good with that."

"I just want you two to be happy with your choices," my mom says sagely.

Griff smiles, shaking his head in amusement. "How about if I got transferred to the Pittsburgh office?"

I'm so shocked my eyes practically bug out of my head. "Doing what?"

Griff ducks his head, rubs at the back of his neck, then gives me a sheepish look. "Well… apparently, our government feels like we should have a direct liaison with Jameson Group because, as the top brass put it, 'They keep poking their noses in everything'."

"You're kidding," I murmur, astonished at this development. Griff will work in Pittsburgh. I can stay at Jameson. And it sounds like we'll actually sort of work together now.

"I think that's cool," Aaron says.

"It's wonderful," my mom exclaims, clasping her hands to her heart.

Griff's attention swings my way. "And you?"

I rise from my chair, move to his side, and drape myself across his lap. Wrapping my arms around his neck, I put my face right in his so we're staring at each other. "Are you sure? I don't want you taking a job you don't want within the FBI just to keep us here in Pittsburgh. I want you to be happy at what you're doing."

"I will be," he assures me. "And part of me being happy is you being happy too. And I know how important your career is to you. How important the people at Jameson are. They're important to me now too."

I can't even respond. Don't care I'm at the table with my mom and kid. I give Griff the biggest, hottest, most promising kiss I've ever bestowed on him, causing us both to see stars when it's all said and done.

As I pull back, he chuckles. "I take it that's a firm 'yes' I should accept the job."

"It's a yes," I confirm, giving him a softer kiss this time.

One that simply says, *I love you.*

My phone starts ringing. I would normally ignore it, but it's Kynan's ringtone. Despite the fact it's after hours, I'm never truly off the clock when the boss calls.

Leaning in, I snag one more kiss before hopping off Griff's lap and moving to the counter to nab my phone.

I answer, lean back against the counter, and listen as Kynan speaks. A chill races up my spine, and my chest starts to constrict. Griff watches me and his expression becomes pinched, because he's reading my body language. My mom and Aaron joke around as they continue to eat, but Griff rises out of his chair and moves toward me.

Kynan finishes by saying, "I need you to come in now."

"I'll be there in half an hour," I assure him before disconnecting the phone.

Griff comes toe to toe with me, bends his head close to mine, and asks, "What is it?"

I look up, almost afraid to even speak the words out loud for fear they might not really be true. My hand goes to his chest, mainly for support.

His heartbeat feels steadying under my fingertips. Still, my voice quavers when I say, "They think they found Malik... and he's alive."

The suspense continues at Jameson Force Security! Preorder Code Name: Ghost (Jameson Force Security, Book #5), coming June 30, 2020!

sawyerbennett.com/bookstore/code-name-ghost

Go here to see other works by Sawyer Bennett:

https://sawyerbennett.com/bookshop

Don't miss another new release by Sawyer Bennett!!! Sign up for her newsletter and keep up to date on new releases, giveaways, book reviews and so much more.

https://sawyerbennett.com/signup

Connect with Sawyer online:

Website: sawyerbennett.com

Twitter: twitter.com/bennettbooks

Facebook: facebook.com/bennettbooks

Instagram: instagram.com/sawyerbennett123

Book+Main Bites:

bookandmainbites.com/sawyerbennett

Goodreads: goodreads.com/Sawyer_Bennett

Amazon: amazon.com/author/sawyerbennett

BookBub: bookbub.com/authors/sawyer-bennett

About the Author

Since the release of her debut contemporary romance novel, Off Sides, in January 2013, Sawyer Bennett has released multiple books, many of which have appeared on the New York Times, USA Today and Wall Street Journal bestseller lists.

A reformed trial lawyer from North Carolina, Sawyer uses real life experience to create relatable, sexy stories that appeal to a wide array of readers. From new adult to erotic contemporary romance, Sawyer writes something for just about everyone.

Sawyer likes her Bloody Marys strong, her martinis dirty, and her heroes a combination of the two. When not bringing fictional romance to life, Sawyer is a chauffeur, stylist, chef, maid, and personal assistant to a very active daughter, as well as full-time servant to her adorably naughty dogs. She believes in the good of others, and that a bad day can be cured with a great work-out, cake, or even better, both.

Sawyer also writes general and women's fiction under the pen name S. Bennett and sweet romance under the name Juliette Poe.

CPSIA information can be obtained
at www.ICGtesting.com
Printed in the USA
LVHW031116280420
654669LV00017B/1742

9 781947 212855